HELL ON WHEELS

Also by G. J. Morgan

BORDER FURY
TRAIL OF DEATH

G. J. Morgan

Hell on Wheels

Futura Publications Limited

A Futura Book

First published in Great Britain in 1975
by Milton House Books

First Futura Publications edition 1975

ISBN 0 8600 7220 7

Printed in Great Britain by
Cox & Wyman Ltd,
London, Reading and Fakenham

Futura Publications Limited
49 Poland Street, London W1A 2LG

CHAPTER ONE

Slade Hollister tensed when the train pulled into Albuquerque and was quickly prepared for its run south along the branch line to El Paso. He remained in his seat, alert and keyed up, while his father, Hard Sam, went through the car to find the conductor. Several cars were shunted away from the train, and couplings clashed sharply as the engine returned, crashing against the remaining single passenger car. There was also a baggage car, two freight cars, a special car with stalls for horses adjoining the express car, and a caboose. Hollister ran his fingers over his jutting chin. Trouble was expected on the next stretch of the run, and trouble-shooting for the Middle & Far Western Railroad was what the Hollisters were paid to do.

Hard Sam returned as the train pulled out of Albuquerque, and he carefully looked over the score of passengers in the car as he made his way back to Slade. At sixty years of age, Hard Sam was coming to the end of his tracks as Railroad Supervisor – chief troubleshooter – and it was unofficially regarded in all railroad circles that Slade would step into his father's boots when the moment arrived for Hard Sam to call it a day.

'No signs of trouble yet!' Sam reported in low tones as he sat down opposite his son. It was evident they were from the same mould. Both were tall, heavy muscled, with strong, open faces and keen blue eyes. Slade's jaw was lean and determined, but his father's was showing age in loose folds of skin and deep creases. Both men were heavily armed, and their manner suggested they were quite capable of handling anything that came up. Sam had a tough reputation, built up over the long years, which he jealously guarded, and Slade was easily emulating his father's endeavours.

'It's a mighty long way to El Paso,' Slade replied. 'I think we'll get what we are here for!' He drew his holstered Colt .45 and blew the dust off the gleaming barrel. His pale blue eyes glinted as he met his father's gaze squarely for a moment. 'It's about time we nailed Drogo Rolph and his boys. They've been in our hair for too long.'

'Rolph is the only reason I'm keeping you out of my job, Slade,' Hard Sam said tightly. 'You know I been offered an Area Manager's desk by Colonel Bill. But me and Drogo Rolph are old enemies, and I ain't quitting until he's got his come-uppance!'

The train clattered through a canyon, thundering between the narrow, confining walls, its whistle shrilling, echoing eerily from the surrounding peaks. It emerged in a high valley where there was rich grass, and Slade narrowed his eyes as he gazed at an adobe ranch house in the distance. The whistle blew again, and as they left the valley the train began to slacken its jolting progress, hitting a curving grade that wound sinuously upwards to cross a trestle bridge spanning a deep gorge.

Hard Sam was uneasy, and it troubled Slade to see his father so. Usually nothing bothered the older man, but it was no easy matter to accept that Drogo Rolph and his men were scheduled to hit this train. Rolph had a terrible reputation in his own spheres of activity, and over the years he had stolen and shot his way to the top of the wanted lists.

The train was moving at a walking pace up the last stretch of the grade, its engine panting heavily, the cars bumping and shunting on the glittering track. Slade saw a buzzard swinging in lazy circles high in the still air. In the distance was a row of mountain peaks, rocky and barren, backed by still higher peaks, red and broken in the sunlight. The sky was brassy, steel-grey and burnished, and heat shimmered into the distance like an unbroken stretch of cool, inviting water.

A movement attracted Slade's narrowed gaze and he jerked his head quickly, to look at the shadow of the train on the ground. The outline of the cars was smooth and plain, but the movement continued, and Slade saw the shadow of a man's figure moving along the top of the car, from the caboose towards the engine.

He drew his sixgun as he attracted his father's attention and pointed out the window. Hard Sam looked, then uttered a low curse.

'I'll take care of the engine,' he directed coldly. 'You go cover the express car, Slade!'

They moved away in opposite directions. Slade went to the rear of the car and left it, climbing quickly to the roof to look around. He saw the man whose shadow he had spotted about to leap onto the coal tender, and turned his attention to the express car behind him. Hard Sam would take care of the front of the train.

The train reached the top of the grade and rumbled across the bridge. They began to pick up speed now, and Slade guessed that the rest of the robbers were not aboard yet.

Slade checked his gun while he clung to the rungs with one hand. A big figure suddenly thrust into view between the car and the coal tender, and he recognized his father. Hard Sam was holding a ready sixgun as he stood up on the catwalk on the roof of the car and steadied himself for a leap onto the coal tender. Slade caught his breath, wishing he had been sent forward. But he glanced backwards at the express car, knowing where his duty lay. The next instant the crash of a shot made him look forward again, and he saw Hard Sam crumpling to the roof of the swaying car, his gun falling from his hand.

Slade climbed onto the roof and started running towards the locomotive. He reached his father's side, but did no more than peer down at Hard Sam in passing. There was a splotch of blood on Sam's shirt front, and the older man's eyes were closed, his face pale and taut.

Slade kept moving, leaping for the coal tender. He could see the fireman standing with his hands raised, the engineer with his hand on the throttle, obviously obeying orders from the stranger who stood on the footplate, a levelled gun in his hand. He was masked, with his black Stetson pulled low over his eyes. Slade lifted his gun a fraction and thumbed off a shot. Gunsmoke blew into his face and he caught the acrid taste of it, his nose wrinkling as he watched his target. The hold-up man was jerking under the powerful impact of the heavy slug, his gun hand falling away, and the fireman lowered his hands and grappled with him, snatching away the gun and turning the muzzle to cover the stranger.

Slade stood for a moment, peering around, looking for more trouble, then turned and went back to where Sam was lying. His father was conscious, trying to pad the bullet wound in his right shoulder. Slade dropped to one knee beside the older man.

7

Sam looked up at him, his lips thin, his eyes glittering.

'I'm okay,' he rapped. 'You nail the sidewinder?'

'He's hit and a prisoner.'

'Good. Get back to the express car and check with the messenger. When I've stopped the bleeding I'll get the prisoner. Keep your eyes lifting, Slade. The rest of the gang will be along here someplace, waiting for the train to stop.'

Slade turned away, moving back along the roof until he reached the express car. The caboose was behind it, and he checked both cars from the outside, unable to get into the express car, which was locked from the inside. He knew the messenger inside would be on his toes and ready for anything, and he crouched on the roof of the caboose, watching either side of the track as the train progressed through the barren countryside.

When he saw movement far ahead he stiffened, and dropped to one knee, his gun coming to hand immediately. There were half a dozen horses at the trackside, and it was obvious that was where the train was supposed to halt. Slade narrowed his eyes, for only one of the horses had a rider. The other five were riderless!

The train began to lose speed. Slade frowned as he peered ahead. Surely they were not going to stop! His father had gone down onto the footplate to take charge of the prisoner. Hard Sam knew better than to stop and fight. They had several thousand dollars in gold bullion aboard. Slade tightened his grip upon his gun and flattened himself upon the roof of the caboose, his pale, glittering eyes watching the lone horseman up ahead.

He heard the sound of the heavy door of the express car sliding open, and inched sideways until he could peer down at the side of it. He saw the black gap of the open doorway of the express car, and a man was standing there, peering out ahead. He was a stranger to Slade.

The train stopped near to the rider and horses, and immediately four men leaped to the ground from the express car. Three of them were carrying gunny sacks bulging with gold. The fourth, a tall, massively built man, was carrying two drawn pistols, and his hands moved ominously as he looked around for

8

trouble. The rider with the horses was coming alongside the track towards the express car.

A gun blasted then, its booming report echoing away across the desolate scenery. Slade saw the rider pitch sideways out of his saddle, and his eyes glinted when he realized that Hard Sam had probably guessed at the true situation and had deliberately stopped the train in order to have some chance of nailing the robbers. The horses came at a run and the robbers ran to meet them.

Slade cut loose with his sixgun, his first shot dropping the nearest of the four men. Two sacks of gold clunked to the ground. The robber holding the two guns swung around, his masked face unreal in the sunlight. Both weapons in his hands exploded, and slivers of wood leaped out of the edge of the roof of the caboose. Slade felt the sharp sting of torn flesh on his left cheek and ducked as he continued to work his gun. His second shot took the armed robber through the left forearm, causing him to drop one of his weapons.

Then the horses arrived, and the robbers grabbed at them. Slade pushed himself backwards and got to his feet, running forward to leap across to the roof of the express car itself. Then he hurled himself flat and bellied forward to peer down at the ground.

Another of the robbers was down, caught by good shooting from the engine, and Slade saw the other two were now mounted and riding fast for cover. He emptied his gun at them, but they were rapidly drawing out of sixgun range. When his hammer clicked against an empty chamber he sat up and reloaded, his face grim, his eyes narrowed and watching the getaway of the two men.

The echoes of the shooting faded slowly, reluctantly, grumbling away into the distance. Slade holstered his gun and climbed from the roof, dropping to the ground beside the track. Hard Sam was coming from the engine, his gun in his hand, a tight grin on his pale face. Heads were peering from many windows.

'Good work,' Sam spoke through stiff lips as he came up. 'I figured you would follow my lead. When I saw that rider ahead, with five empty saddles with him, I guessed the robbers were already aboard. There'll be hell to pay over this, Slade.'

'We'll worry about that later. Can you handle this end of it now, Sam?'

'Sure. What are you planning?'

Slade looked in the direction the two escaping robbers had taken. He pointed after them.

'This is the nearest we've come to putting a crimp in Rolph's plans,' he said. 'I figure to unload my hoss and take out after him.'

Slade turned away and walked to the special car, opening the door and dropping the loading ramp. He climbed in and saddled up his black horse, then led the animal out, swinging immediately into the saddle. He checked his supplies before moving away, and then rode off in the tracks the two escaping robbers had left.

Sweat poured down Slade's face as he rode through the breezeless sunlight of noon. He followed the tracks left by two running horses, and when he approached the first line of cover he slowed cautiously, half expecting a bullet to pluck him from his saddle. Away from the railroad track this was a land largely unfrequented by whites, virtually without water. The land was broken, rough, hostile, sullen, brooding. The silence was so intense it seemed to hurt the ears. The sun glare was brilliant to the point of blinding unaccustomed eyes. But Slade was inured to the heat and the harsh realities. At thirty-two, he had sided his father for the past ten years, had seen a number of men killed in the course of handling Railroad Business; had killed seven men over the years in relentless pursuit of duty.

The trail emerged from the canyon, turned north for three miles, then entered a draw that swung east, then south. In the background the mountains reared up majestically, with great walls of ridges stretching away monotonously. As he rode, Slade watched for movement, for the glint of sunlight upon metal, for any sign that would betray the presence of an ambusher who had dropped back to watch for pursuit.

When he reached the point where the two tracks separated he reined up and dismounted to give his horse a breather. For long minutes he stared off to north, then south, wondering which of the two men had taken the sacks of bullion, guessing that the gold would travel with Drogo Rolph himself. He decided that the horse moving southwards made the deeper tracks, which signified much more than the weight of an ordinary man.

Sweat was stale upon him by the time he reached high ground and left the broken land behind. Tracks still pointed the way for him, mocking him with their silent presence. He crossed a long ridge of gravel and sand which was sparsely dotted with prickly pear and bear grass, and when he reached the summit he paused, although he knew he could be spotted by the man he was following. He dismounted again and moved a few yards from his horse, turning very slowly as he studied the ground. There was a faint breeze now, and it felt almost cold through his sweat soaked shirt. Then he saw what he was looking for! Far away a wisp of dust hung motionless in still air at the entrance to a canyon. The tracks led in the same direction, and he loosened his sixgun in its holster and went on.

When he reached the mouth of the canyon he saw that the tracks had been blotted out. But it did not matter! The hanging dust had pointed out his quarry's direction. Dismounting, Slade left his horse in cover and went forward on foot, his big, husky figure flitting from rock to rock as he went through the canyon entrance. When he saw the glint of water, the stretch of fairly good grass, he nodded to himself. He was not surprised when he finally glimpsed the shack that was standing back against an overhang of rock.

It took him a long time to approach the shack under cover, moving patiently, crawling, snaking forward silently, careful not to raise dust or alert the two horses grazing quietly some twenty yards beyond the ramshackle building. His hands itched as he drew his gun and prepared to close in upon the shack. He slithered forward on his belly, making for the rear of the building, staying clear of the open doorway and the two glassless windows in front.

He heard voices, and one of them was sharp and shrill, feminine. Slade eased to one knee, careful to prevent his shadow being cast against the wall of the shack, for there were many cracks in the sun-baked woodwork and he knew he could easily be spotted. He moved into the shadows at the rear, coming erect and taking a deep breath.

Passing around the rear of the shack, Slade reached the far side. Then he heard the sound of a slap, and a string of un-ladylike curses from the feminine voice.

11

'I'm not going to San Blanca, and you can keep your hands off me, you saddle bum! You go keep that appointment with Drogo, and tell him goodbye for me. I'm through. I'm getting out of here, and if I never set eyes on any of this bunch again I'll be happy.'

Slade moved towards a glassless window, lifting his pistol. He peered into the shack, saw a man and woman standing close together, and covered them.

'Hold it!' he snapped. 'Get your hands up and be quick about it. Lady, get away from him.'

A shocked silence followed, and both man and woman turned to stare at him. Slade almost smiled at the identical expressions which dawned slowly, but in the next instant the man was grabbing the woman and reaching for his gun.

Slade fired instantly, almost before he was aware of the action. The big .45 blasted raucously in the close confines of the shack, and gunsmoke plumed across the dim interior. The man took the heavy bullet in the head before he had completed his move to grab the girl, and he went sprawling backwards, to fall in an untidy heap, leaving the girl wide eyed and paralysed in shock. She stared at Slade through the gunsmoke, her face taut, her pale eyes narrowed, and as he watched her for a moment, Slade was conscious of a sense of disappointment. The man he had just killed was not Drogo Rolph.

CHAPTER TWO

Slade moved around the shack and entered by the doorway. The girl did not move. She stared at Slade with wide blue eyes, and he paused, his lips compressed, taking a good look at her, wondering if he had ever seen her before. She was tall, coming almost up to his shoulder, and he stood three inches over six feet. Her hair was long and blonde, reaching almost to her shoulders, and the blue dress she was wearing was out of place in a desolate shack, more in keeping with one of the rowdier saloons back in Big Bend, he decided.

'Anyone else around?' he demanded, and she shook her head wordlessly.

'I'm Slade Hollister.' He paused, watching her keenly. 'My name mean anything to you?' He saw her shrug, and continued: 'This man was with Drogo Rolph and four others. They held up the noon train to El Paso.'

'What happened?' She was beginning to recover from her shock. Now there were two tiny spots of colour in her high cheeks. Her blue eyes were narrowed and filled with calculation.

'Three of them were killed, one taken prisoner, and this one and Rolph got away. Rolph took one of my slugs through his left forearm.' He paused again, watching her reactions, studying the situation. 'You're Rolph's girl, huh? You're supposed to meet him now in San Blanca! Well you ain't gonna keep that appointment. I'll be there instead. Come on outside. I want to check over the horse that hombre rode in on.'

He glanced down at the dead man, his lips tightening, his expression hardening a fraction as his narrowed blue eyes took in the extent of the wound his heavy .45 slug had caused. The bullet had taken the man through the forehead, and a thin trickle of blood showed around the purpled entry wound. The exit of the slug had jerked the man's hat off, and it lay beside the body, saturated with heavy stains and part of the contents of the skull.

There was a sack of gold slung from the saddlehorn of the horse the robber and ridden in on, and the girl watched silently as Slade checked it. She stared sullenly at the gold bars that glinted dully in the sunlight, and when Slade looked up quickly and surprised the expression on her face he grinned tightly.

'What's your name?'

'Maisie Clapham!' There was defiance in her gaze.

'You came out of a saloon someplace, I guess. So now you got yourself into a lot of trouble, Maisie. It is against the law to consort with known outlaws.'

'I ain't done a blame thing that's against the law, except mebbe cook for those skunks. And they didn't treat me good for my pains! Good thing you caught up with them, Mr Hollister. I heard about you.'

'Not me, mebbe. My Pa, I expect,' he retorted. 'He's Hard Sam Hollister.'

'Everyone's heard about Hard Sam Hollister.' She nodded slowly. 'Drogo always said there was only one man standing between him and a fortune, and that was Hard Sam guarding the railroad company's assets.'

'What else can you tell me about Drogo Rolph?' he asked.

She smiled slowly, shaking her head. 'No deal. If I opened my trap to you and Drogo got to hear about it I'd be as good as dead. Do you know Drogo, mister?'

'No, but I've heard all about him,' Slade said. 'Now tell me about his other hideouts. Where would he make for now?'

'You heard that I am supposed to ride to San Blanca to meet him. But if you do go there you'll be wasting your time. He'll know before he rides in whether I'm there or not, and if I ain't then he won't show.'

'So you'd better ride in there and let him figure nothing is wrong,' he suggested, and she was shaking her head before he finished speaking.

'No deal.'

'Okay. So you'd better saddle up and get out of here. Don't let me catch you mixed up with this bunch again, Maisie, or it'll go bad for you. Beat it, and be gone before I'm ready to ride.'

She turned away immediately, hurrying into the shack, and Slade followed her, careful to collect all the weapons he could

14

find. He watched while she put some dresses and other items into a sack, and when she was ready to leave he motioned to the dead man stiffening on the dirt floor.

'What was his name, Maisie?' he demanded.

'Joe Wade. He's got a mother living Sonora way. Now can I go?'

'So long.' He went to the door of the shack and stood watching her as she saddled and rode out. When she was out of range he turned to the grim task of burying his victim. An hour later, with the sack of gold tied to his cantle, he rode out himself, making for Big Bend, the Area Headquarters of the railroad.

It took Slade three days to reach Big Bend, and on the morning of the fourth day, travel stained and gaunted, he reined up on a ridge and stared down at the town. He did not like Big Bend, not for the small town itself but because Frank Burden, the Area Manager, had his headquarters here. He gigged his mount and they started down the long slope, eventually reaching the mouth of the street, and he turned off to the right and rode into the livery barn, turning the black over to the liveryman with explicit instructions for its care.

He carried the sack of bullion in his left hand as he walked along the boardwalk for some three blocks. Crossing the street, Slade entered the sheriff's office, pausing in the doorway to look around with a glitter in his blue eyes. He had no time for Sheriff Barnes, who failed to do his duty with the enthusiasm and capable violence that it demanded. Barnes preferred to sit in the back room at the Buckaroo's Bar playing poker till all hours, leaving the law dealing to his deputy, young Billy Dainton. It was Dainton seated behind the desk, and the youth looked up alertly, then got to his feet when he saw Slade.

'Glad to see you back, Slade!' Dainton said. 'Did you come up with Rolph?'

Slade shook his head and made a brief report.

'Joe Wade, huh?' Dainton shook his head. 'Can't say I ever heard of him. Pity it wasn't one of the other members of the gang, like Mulie Johnson or Ned Bunch or Bull Seymour! Or Rolph himself!'

'Where's Barnes?' Slade cut in. 'Tell him what I've said. Send a wire to the deputy over at San Blanca and say that Drogo Rolph is expected to show up around there at any time, trying to contact a girl named Maisie Clapham. How's Hard Sam?'

'He's okay! That wound in his shoulder will keep him out of action for some time, but he was walking around town yesterday, I saw.'

'I'll see you later.' Slade took a fresh grip on the sack of bullion and departed, going on along the sidewalk towards the depot. A shout echoed across the street, and Slade turned as he heard his name called. A tight grin touched his firm lips when he recognized his father standing in front of the batwings of the Silver Concho saloon. Hard Sam was dressed in a dark grey store suit and a pale grey Stetson, and he was wearing his sixgun left-handed.

'Glad to see you got back, son,' Sam said thickly. 'Looks like you added to our success. Did you get Rolph?'

Slade gave his story, and saw Sam's face lose some of its pleasure, but the older man listened to the terse report, nodding his approval, his blue eyes glinting with pleasure as Slade described the killing of Joe Wade.

'Good work, Slade,' Sam commented at the end of it. 'You did good. But Drogo Rolph sure has a barn full of luck staked out somewhere. You run that sack of gold into the bank and then get along home and clean up. I have to tell you that as soon as you're able you've got to go talk with Burden.'

'Now what have I done?' Slade smiled, but there was no mirth in him as he thought about the Area Manager. Frank Burden was a dangerous man where his wife Lola was concerned, and Burden figured, mistakenly, that Slade was one of the men who had been having a good time with Lola.

Sam turned away, and Slade went on to the bank, depositing the bullion. Then he went along to the little house at the far end of the street, opposite the railroad depot, where he lived with his father. He went in at the gate, and was called again. He paused and swung around, to find Frank Burden coming across the street towards him.

'It's about time you got in, Hollister,' Burden rapped. He was a big, heavy-set man with a long, fleshy face and jutting jaw. His long nose was knife-ridged, his mouth a tight slit, and his narrowed brown eyes sparkled with challenge and dislike. Thick black hair waved back over his broad skull, and it was grey at the temples. He wore a white shirt and a black string tie, but no coat, and his right hand was resting against his right thigh, where a .45 Colt was holstered. 'Why didn't you come right over to my office and make your report? How long you been in town? How come you figure it is more important to grab a drink before coming to see me?'

'I don't have to report to you, Burden,' Slade retorted in cold tones. 'Hard Sam is my boss and I've just spoken to him. If you want to know why I took so long to get back here then go talk to him, and check with the bank on the bullion I brought back.'

'You caught up with those outlaws?'

'Sam will give you my report,' Slade answered softly. 'I've just got in after four days on the trail. I'm gonna take a bath and change into clean clothes. Then I'll walk across to your office and report for duty.'

'I'll talk to you now,' Burden grated. 'I don't want to have to see you twice in the same day. I got news for you, Hollister. I have been ordered by the Vice-President, Colonel Bill Gomer, to inform you that because your father has been promoted to Area Manager you are to be offered the job of Chief Supervisor in his place. Do you accept?'

Slade looked into the Area Manager's dark eyes, seeing something of the emotional turmoil in the brain beyond, and he could feel a pang of pity for the older man. Frank Burden had been a railroad man all his life, and at fifty he had a good reputation at his back, but two years ago he had married Lola, aged thirty-two, and after a brief spell of happiness he had discovered his wife's many weaknesses numbered infidelity amongst them. It had changed Burden. He killed one man and wounded several more before he managed to curb Lola's appetites, and he was still ready to lift his gun when his jealousy got the better of him. He suspected Slade was one of the men who betrayed him and, although his suspicions had not been put into so many words, Slade was aware that he could have trouble from this situation.

'I heard that you figure Phil Brady should get the job when Hard Sam retires,' Slade said.

'He's been a troubleshooter on the railroad five years longer than you, and built himself a good reputation.' There was a sneer in Burden's tones, 'But you got a father ahead of you, and

I guess it's Brady's hard luck that Colonel Bill figures the sun shines out of your eyes.'

'I'll take the job,' Slade said. 'But before I start handling this situation I want to get something straight with you. You hate my guts because you figure I've taken advantage of your wife. That's about it, huh?'

Burden tensed, clenching his big hands, and his jawline bunched as he gritted his teeth. His dark eyes glittered as emotion fed jealousy and hatred through to his mind.

'Damn you, Hollister,' he rasped, 'if you figure to have some fun at my expense. Hell, I've killed a man for Lola.'

'And you figure I'm just the kind of man she goes for. Slade spoke sharply. 'I never think of her, Burden. She never crosses my path and I don't care one way or another about her. You better get that straight before we start working together. I'm a Company man, and outside of the railroad I got no interests. I never looked twice at your wife.'

'You're lying! Okay, so you've brought it out into the open. You figure to make me believe that you don't fancy Lola, like all the other men around here. But she's been dropping hints about some man, and I got the conclusion it's you she's talking about.'

'You're wrong, and you better let it drop there, Burden. We've both got a tough job to do, and from my side you better know that I've taken all I want of your suspicions. It's getting so other folk are beginning to think there's a fire under the smoke you're raising.'

'I told you we'll work together,' Burden retorted, turning away. 'I'd like to talk to you in my office when you've cleaned up. I'll be there until noon.'

'I'll see you in an hour,' Slade replied, and went into the house.

He dressed in a black broadcloth store suit and buckled his cartridge belt around his waist, tying down the holster around his right thigh. He tossed his dusty trail clothes into a basket, leaving them for the cleaning woman to wash, and while he stood before the jagged piece of mirror that Hard Sam had salvaged from a train wreck years before, tying his string tie, he heard the front door click shut. He turned instantly, his gun leaping into his hand, and there was a frown on his face

18

as he reholstered the weapon and went to see who had entered. He figured his nerves must be suffering, the way he had pulled the gun without thinking about it. But he had a shock when he saw the woman standing just inside the house. It was Lola Burden.

'What are you trying to do?' he demanded angrily. 'Aren't you satisfied with the trouble you've heaped on Frank's plate? I was talking to him half an hour ago. He figures I'm the man you're seeing on the quiet, Lola.'

'I wish you were, Slade,' she said vibrantly, coming to stand before him, lifting her long, slender hands to his wide shoulders. She was tall and slender, small-waisted. Her wide, sensuous lips were curved in a mocking smile under a small, straight nose, and her dark eyes gleamed luminously, afire with hidden emotion which she seemed to be able to turn on at will. Her skin was dark and smooth, unblemished, and her manner suggested that she was keenly aware of her beauty and what it did to the men around her. She was dressed in a voluminous split riding skirt, with a white loose shirt, unbuttoned at the neck, under a bolero jacket. Her jet black long hair showed under a flat-crowned hat. She pushed against him until he caught the intangible smell of her perfume, and he clenched his teeth and backed off a step.

'Stop that, Lola.'

'I'm not doing anything, Slade,' she protested, her eyes wide in simulated surprise and innocence. 'I heard that Frank came to see you, and I'm looking for him.'

'Cut it out,' he retorted. 'I've got you pegged for what you are, Lola, and you know it. Burden told me you've been dropping hints about the man you're seeing on the quiet, and he suspects me. You're doing it deliberately, huh? You're hoping to get Frank going at me so I'll be forced to kill him. That's what you want, isn't it? You want Burden dead so you'll be free of him, and you don't care who does the dirty work for you.'

'I love Frank.' She spoke quietly, and but the fact that he knew how she played around with other men, Slade might have believed her. 'I want him out of this area, Slade. You can help me. Discredit him in some way so he has to move on. He could take the northern area, where they are sending Hard Sam. I'd do anything to get him away from Big Bend.' She pressed forward again, thrusting herself into his arms, and Slade looked at her smooth throat where the shirt was unbuttoned, saw the hint of shadow there marking the beginning swell of her breasts. She swayed towards him, touching him, and he clenched his teeth and pivoted away from her, moving angrily to the door.

'Go on back to your husband, Lola,' he said, jerking open the door. 'Stay well clear of me. I've got enough trouble on my hands without you adding to it. And stop hinting to Frank that I could be your lover. If he comes at me with a gun I might have to kill him.'

CHAPTER THREE

Slade was thoughtful when he left the house and crossed the street to the depot. He went along to the Area Manager's office and shouldered through the doorway, pausing before a low-railed barrier, then thrusting through the thigh-high swing gate to approach the huge roll-top desk angled across a corner by the window. Frank Burden sat at the desk, his shirt sleeves rolled up to the elbows, revealing brawny arms that were heavily covered with long black hair.

'So you decided to show up,' he said.

Slade fixed Burden with an unblinking stare. 'Before we go any further let's get one thing straight,' he said softly. 'Cut out this tough attitude towards me, Burden. If we are to work together then leave personalities out of it.'

A shadow crossed Burden's face, and for a moment he looked ready to leap up and start fighting, but he swallowed noisily and clenched his hands.

'Let's get down to business.' Slade's pale gaze flickered to the maps on the wall. 'There are three men working under me in this area, right?'

'Harry Kelleher, Phil Brady and young Jim Longley,' Burden said grudgingly.

'Where are they now and what are they chasing up?'

'Harry went over to Las Corros three days ago to check on some stolen freight from the yards. Phil Brady went to Hobbsburg for the same reason.'

'And Jim?'

'I sent him to watch for Rolph's gang around San Blanca.'

'You did.' Slade tensed. 'That could be a break for us.' He went on to explain about Maisie Clapham. 'If she's run to San Blanca like I expect then Rolph will show up there in a day or so. But I don't figure Longley is man enough to handle Rolph on his own.'

'He draws a troubleshooter's pay so he'll have to learn to handle the chores,' Burden muttered.

'I couldn't get to San Blanca in time,' Slade mused. 'We won't have a train going there until Friday. Kelleher is nearest at Las Corros. Let's send him a wire telling him to get over to San Blanca. He's a veteran, and he can take charge.'

'I'll wire Longley as well, telling him to stand by.' Burden forgot his personal feelings for a moment. He looked steadily into Slade's pale eyes. 'I figure you're gonna have some trouble with Brady when he learns you've been promoted over his head.'

'I'll worry about that when the time comes,' Slade retorted. 'Right now my only concern is getting Rolph and his gang. They're causing more trouble than all the other badmen put together.'

'I had a report yesterday from Chain Becker at end of track on the spur line being built to Jules Crossing. The Overland Freight Company is gonna be put out of business by the Railroad Company, and the chances are that they won't give in without a fight. There's a shanty town springing up at end of track, and a couple of tent saloons have arrived. Becker says he's getting trouble from the men. They're drinking and gambling when they should be working.'

'I'll go out there tomorrow,' Slade said instantly. 'Anything else?'

'Not right now. But I'll keep in touch with you.'

Slade left the office and went along the street to the saloon, pushing through the batwings and crossing the sawdust-strewn floor to the bar where his father was standing. Hard Sam called for whisky and a beer for Slade, then looked his son in the eyes.

'You talked to Frank Burden?' the older man demanded, and tightened his lips when Slade nodded silently. 'So you know you've got my job,' he rasped.

'Your old job,' Slade corrected. 'You're taking over as Area Manager north of Burden's area.'

'And Drogo Rolph is operating in this area,' Sam replied. He watched Slade while his son drained his glass of whisky, and shook his head when Slade met his gaze above the rim of his beer glass. 'You've got to forget everything else and make an all-out effort to put an end to Rolph's activities. With him and his boys out of the way you'll have an easy time of it, but while Rolph is on the loose you'll be run ragged, Slade.'

'I know it, and I'm gonna concentrate on him.' Slade drained his glass. He explained what he had done about San Blanca, and Sam nodded approvingly.

They left the saloon and paused on the boardwalk. Slade looked around the street. There were a number of saddle horses at hitching rails in front of various buildings, and a buckboard or two in front of the general store. A rider was coming into town, and Slade narrowed his eyes to see who it was.

'That's Phil Brady coming,' Hard Sam reported. 'He went to Hobbsburg to check on a freight theft from the yard there.'

Brady spotted them and changed direction, coming across the street to rein up at the edge of the sidewalk. He sat his saddle, cuffing back his battered black Stetson, knocking off some of the thick dust clinging to him. He was a tall, muscular man with a tanned face and secretive brown eyes. His checked shirt, levis and cartridge belt were dull under a thick layer of dust. He had a square jaw, a chunky body with wide, powerful shoulders and heavy arms, and his hair, showing under the brim of his hat, was black and greasy.

'Howdy, Sam?' he greeted in dry, rasping tones. His dark eyes flickered to Slade, and he nodded briefly but did not speak. 'Heard what you did to the Rolph gang four days ago. But it wasn't enough, huh? You should have nailed Rolph!'

'You don't have to report to me any more, Phil,' said Sam. 'I got winged in the shoot-out with Rolph's boys and Colonel Bill has decided it's time I called it a day. I'm getting that desk job they've been promising me for years, and Slade here has taken over my job. He's your boss from now on.'

There was a silence that seemed oppressive in the bright sunlight. Slade, watching Brady intently, admired the man's control, for there was not the slightest change of expression at what must have been bad news. Brady had been half expecting the big saddle to go his way when Hard Sam Hollister retired.

His dark eyes glinted as he looked Slade over, and then he nodded, smiled sourly.

'It comes as no surprise,' he commented. 'It's always handy to have pull in upper places. I guess it was on the cards for the job to stay in the same family.'

'I figure you know like I do that Colonel Bill wouldn't pick a man because of his connections,' Sam said sharply. 'On the railroad the man who deserves the job gets it.'

'That's like saying I ain't done my duty right in the last fifteen years.'

'You know better than that.' Sam shook his head. 'You're a hard man, Phil, and you've done a good job, but over the past three years Slade had the advantage over you in that he worked closely with me, and he does know my job as well as if not better than me.'

'I don't need explanations,' Brady said. He looked up at Slade, who was watching him intently. 'What about some orders? You got something for me to do?'

'Write out your report on Hobbsburg,' Slade said instantly. 'Get cleaned up and we'll talk later. I'll see you down at the depot at four.'

Brady nodded and lifted his right hand to cuff down his hat. He grinned as he rode on, and went back across the street and continued to the depot. Slade watched his progress in silence, and Sam shook his head and sighed harshly.

'Watch out for him, Slade. He's deep and hard to figure. There's always been something back of him that I didn't cotton to. I never could put my finger on it, but that don't mean it ain't there. Walk careful when he's around, and don't let him get downwind of you.'

They ate at Kate's Diner, and afterwards Slade went along to the law office. There was still no sign of Sheriff Barnes, but the deputy was dozing in the seat behind the desk. Slade stood for a moment staring at the youngster, then shook his head and went on his way.

He met Phil Brady on the sidewalk outside the Buckaroo's Bar, and Brady looked as if he would not stop, but Slade stepped in front of the man and forced him to halt.

'I'd like to have a talk with you, Phil,' he said. 'Let me buy you a drink.'

24

Brady looked as if he would refuse, and for a moment their gazes met. Then Brady nodded and turned aside into the bar.

'What's on your mind?'

'I'd like to know what's on yours, Phil,' Slade countered. 'We are gonna have to work together, and mebbe trust our lives to each other. I got the feeling something's been biting you mighty hard lately, and we'd better straighten it out.'

Brady grinned slowly as he shook his head. 'I got no axe to grind, Slade. You figure mebbe I'm disappointed about you getting Hard Sam's job. Well I figured it that way a long time ago, although others seemed to think I had a chance. But I'm happy with my job the way it is, and if they had offered me Sam's place I reckon I might have turned it down.'

'Maybe I've got too good an imagination, Phil,' Slade said. 'So let's get back to business. Have you picked up anything at all about Rolph's gang? There were new faces with him on that raid we smashed. Mulie Johnson wasn't there, and neither were Ned Bunch and Bull Seymour. I'm wondering what's happening to them.'

'I haven't heard a thing,' Brady said instantly. He met Slade's gaze for a moment. 'We're gonna have to get Rolph before we think of anything else. He's getting away with too much, and a thing like that is bad for our business and good for the outlaws.'

'I agree with you, and that's why I'm gonna concentrate upon Rolph and his boys. I figure the best thing we could do is set a trap for them.' Slade's voice was low pitched and raw. 'We could put it about that a large gold shipment is going through.'

'Perhaps we don't have to spread the word,' Brady said thoughtfully.

'What do you mean?'

'Hasn't it struck you that Rolph always seems to know which trains to hold up?' There was a glint in Brady's dark eyes. 'He never picks the empty ones. The way I see it, Rolph is picking up information from someone connected with the Company.'

'That's a nasty thought.' Slade shook his head. 'There can't be too many men with the kind of information that Rolph would need.'

'Then it should be fairly simple to check up on them.'

'I'll have a word with Hard Sam.' Slade finished his beer. He started to get up, but changed his mind and looked into Brady's face. 'You must have been thinking about this for some time, Phil,' he suggested. 'Do you have any ideas who could be at the back of it?'

'What about Burden?'

Slade shook his head without considering the suggestion.

'I'd stake my life on Frank Burden,' he said.

'Do that and you could wind up dead,' Brady retorted, getting to his feet. 'I've given you something to think about,' he remarked. 'It's your job to do the thinking now. Let's hope you'll come up to Colonel Bill's expectations.'

He turned and departed, and Slade stared after him, feeling out of his depth, filled with an uncertainty he had not known before. He needed to talk everything over with Hard Sam. He wanted advice and help, and his first job as Chief Supervisor had not started yet. He smiled wryly as he sweated along the sidewalk. He always had to do things the hard way. It was not enough that he had Drogo Rolph to fix. He had to get himself a couple of enemies amongst the railroad men, and two worse enemies than Frank Burden and Phil Brady he could not imagine. Burden was burning up over his wife's infidelity and Brady was the smooth kind who never let his real feelings show. Of the two, Brady could prove the more dangerous.

Crossing the wide street, Slade did not use his customary caution. He failed to check his surroundings as Hard Sam had taught him. He failed to glimpse the flicker of sunlight on a long metal barrel that protruded from an open hotel window, and his first intimation of trouble was the swift, paralysing strike of a bullet punching through the top of his left shoulder.

Simultaneously came the sharp crack of the shot, and Slade fell instantly, reaching for his .45, dragging it clear of the heavy leather holster as he fought the shock and confusion that struck at him. His blue eyes were narrowed as he peered around, knowing full well that a second shot would be speeding at him within a few seconds, and he was out in the open, like a fly on a window pane. His shoulder was stiffly numb, with stabs of pure agony lancing through it with pulsating beat. He could feel blood dribbling down his chest as he searched for the tell-tale puff of gunsmoke that would betray the position of his ambusher, and the fast moving echoes of that first heavy shot were chasing themselves out to town limits. Along the street a number of dogs were barking furiously at the raucous disturbance. Slade gritted his teeth.

Then all hell broke loose.

CHAPTER FOUR

Time always seemed to stand still for Slade when action struck, but now events came fast and furious. He caught a glimpse of movement at an open window in the hotel, saw sunlight flicker on the blued barrel of a rifle, but as he swung his sixgun to return fire another weapon cut at him from an alley farther along the street. A bullet smacked the ground a foot in front of him, spurting dust as the slug itself screeched away in ricochet. The second shot almost threw Slade off mental balance, but he sent two shots at the hotel window, his gun booming quickly, gunsmoke spurting. A second shot struck the street scant inches in front of him from the second ambusher, and he blinked rapidly as dust hit his eyes. He rolled over, clenching his teeth against the pain that stabbed through his left shoulder, and he caught his breath as he searched for the second man against him.

Gunsmoke was forming a cloud in an alley mouth, and Slade pushed himself to one knee, looking again at the hotel window. A pane of glass had been shattered by one of his bullets, and the man with the rifle was no longer visible. Slade got to his feet and started running for the spot. He was breathing hard by the time he reached the alley, and he saw it was empty. Glancing around the street, he saw men beginning to emerge from the buildings to find out the cause of the shooting. He started along the alley, running fast, his big gun ready for instant use in his right hand. Reaching the far end of the alley, he saw a rider making it away across the back lots at a dead run, and lifted his gun. But he refrained from shooting. The man was already out of effective pistol shot, and it would be wasting lead to try and nail him.

He turned and ran towards the back of the hotel, his blue eyes narrowed in determination. He found a couple of men coming out of the doorway as he reached it, and his big gun lifted to cover them. But they were local men, and he ignored their excited questions, pushing past them

28

to enter the building and make a dash up the rear stairs.

He knew which room the shots had been fired from, and went to it, reloading his gun as he did so. The door was open and he could see the interior without entering. There was a discarded rifle lying on the floor by the open window, and shards of glass lay on the window sill. Slade sighed heavily as he paused and studied the scene, but a faint ray of hope touched his mind when he saw blood on the floor by the rifle. His shots had hit his ambusher.

As he turned round to go back down to the street Billy Dainton appeared in the doorway, a gun in his hand. The youngster's face was filled with excitement, his eyes blazing.

'What in hell happened, Slade?' he demanded.

'Two jaspers used me for a target,' Slade replied, still moving. 'The one who was in here with that rifle has been hit. The other took out across the back lots. I figure to go after him.'

'But you're bleeding,' Dainton protested. 'It looks bad, Slade.'

'It'll wait until I get back.' Slade moved through the doorway. 'Check out the town for a wounded man, Billy. I can't give you any description to work on, but I put a bullet mark on him somewhere and he may need medical attention.'

Without wasting further time, Slade went down the front stairs and left the hotel. There was a crowd gathering in the street, and Hard Sam was coming along the sidewalk.

'You've been hit,' Sam said when he arrived. He opened Slade's shirt and examined the wound. 'It ain't bad, but you better get it fixed right away. What happened?'

'Walk with me to the Doc's and I'll tell you,' Slade replied.

They pushed through the crowd, and Slade explained what had happened as they pounded the boardwalk to the Doc's house. The crowd followed at a distance, and as they passed the Buckaroo's Bar Sheriff Barnes appeared in the doorway, holding some playing cards in his hand. Slade grinned, for the sheriff ought to have been holding his gun. Barnes, a big, bluff man with dark hair and eyes, stared at the Hollisters with reproof in his expression.

'Was it you two disturbing the peace?' he demanded.

Slade explained what had happened, and Barnes shrugged.

'I guess you two have made a lot of enemies amongst the badmen,' he said, turning to go back into the Bar. 'It's an occupational risk we peace officers have to take.' They entered the doctor's office, and Doc Layton, a small, oldish man with a greying goatee and long side-whiskers, soon cleaned Slade's wound and bandaged it.

'Try to rest that arm, Slade,' he warned.

'Sure,' Slade said, smiling. 'I'm gonna ride out now on the track of the man who shot me.'

'Didn't you get a look at either man?' Hard Sam demanded.

Slade shook his head. 'No. It could have been anyone. But I winged one of them, so if you are called out to treat someone for a gunshot wound, Doc, you might let us know, huh?'

'I'll surely do that,' Layton replied.

They left the doctor's office and Billy Dainton appeared, still excited by the shooting.

'I've sent a man out on the trail of that rider,' he said. 'I would have gone myself but the sheriff is off duty and I got to stick around town.'

'That's okay,' Slade said. 'I'll be riding out myself. I need to pick up that ambusher, whoever he is.'

'I'll ride with you,' Hard Sam said.

'You better stick around town,' Slade told him. 'We need someone here to handle that situation over in San Blanca. Will you take care of this end while I try to get that ambusher?'

'Okay.' Hard Sam sighed. 'You're the chief troubleshooter now, and what you say goes. I'll be standing by around the depot in case anything comes up. I got wires sent off to Kelleher and the deputy in San Blanca. If Rolph shows up there he'll get a warm reception.'

Slade saddled up and fifteen minutes later he was riding out of Big Bend.

He took up the trail, following the tracks left by the ambusher and the posse man Billy Dainton had sent on ahead, and when he was clear of town, Slade settled his mind to the job in hand. There was nothing he could do about San Blanca. He had taken all possible steps to ensure that Rolph would be caught if he ventured into the town. But he could not be in two places at once, and instead of sitting around town wasting time until news came through he could be better employed trying to get to the bottom of the attack upon him.

For two hours he rode steadily, following two sets of prints, until in the distance he espied a rider coming towards him. When they drew nearer he saw the rider leading a horse, and there was an ominous, blanket-covered shape slung across the saddle of the led animal. Slade saw the rider was a townsman who usually rode out as a posseman for the law, and when they met the posseman, a heavy, dour type, grinned his satisfaction.

'Howdy, Slade,' he greeted. 'You nailed this hombre. Found him on the ground with his horse nearby. He was dead. You got him through the chest.'

Slade frowned as he dismounted to go look at the face of the dead man. He had not fired at the rider who escaped from the alley, so this had to be the man who shot at him from the hotel. He lifted a corner of the blanket and then grasped the black hair of the dead man, twisting the face to peer at it, and a spasm of surprise hit him when he recognized the stiffening features.

'Got any idea who it is?' the posseman demanded.

'Yeah, I know him!' Slade spoke through stiff lips. 'It's Ned Bunch, one of Drogo Rolph's gang.'

'I heard of Bunch, but never set eyes on him before today. How come he was in town taking shots at you, Slade?'

'It's a fact that none of Rolph's old bunch was in on that last robbery we foiled a few days ago,' Slade said, dropping the blanket back into place and returning to his horse. 'Take him back into town and report to Hard Sam about this, will you? I've got some chores to take care of, and I won't be able to get at the second ambusher from here. Tell my father I'm riding on over the mountains to end of track on the Jules Crossing spur line. I'm due to go there tomorrow anyways, and I want to get it over with before coming back to check on the San Blanca incident. Tell Sam he can send any messages for me to end of track.'

'Okay, and good luck. There's a reward for Ned Bunch, ain't there?'

'Seven hundred dollars,' Slade said.

'It's yours. You nailed him. All I had to do was pick him up.' There was an eagerness in the posseman's voice, and Slade grinned.

'Okay, Dan,' he said. 'You take two hundred of that reward, huh?'

'Thanks, Slade, and I hope we can do some more business together. I sure wish I could get in on Rolph himself, or some of the others of his gang.'

'You might be able to at that,' Slade said as he swung into his saddle and started away. 'Be seeing you, Dan.'

Slade was thoughtful as he continued, a lonely figure crossing the barren wastes that stretched to the nearby mountains. There was a pointed question in his mind that clamoured for an answer, and he kept frowning as he tried to find the reasons why outlaws should risk riding into town in an attempt to nail him.

He camped that night in a dry wash, ate cold food and bedded down, sleeping easily, and when the sun came up next morning he awakened instantly, ate, and broke camp. By noon he was following a precarious trail through a pass in the mountains, aiming for Las Corros on the farther side. From there the spur line stretched out towards Jules Crossing, and Slade knew he would have his hands full with the problems Chain Becker had on his plate.

Becker was construction manager of the spur line, and bossed the end of track. If he had trouble with tent saloons and gamblers and could not handle them then it had to be a tough situation, and Slade knew he was getting all the hardest chores at the outset in his career as chief troubleshooter.

It was evening when Slade rode into Las Corros, and his whole left side from shoulder to waist was stiff and painful as he dismounted wearily outside the stable. His shadow was long upon the ground as he glanced around at the wide, rutted street of the little town, and desert dust was like grey gunpowder on his clothes. He took his saddlebags and rifle and walked along the sidewalk to the one-storey adobe-built hotel, still sweating in the last of the day's heat.

He registered and collected a key to one of the rooms, locking himself in, cleaning his sixgun and oiling it before washing and shaving. Then he put on a clean shirt, beat the dust out of his pants and vest and went for a meal. He felt more civilized after supper, and went out to sit on the bench in front of the hotel in the growing darkness of approaching night.

The breeze had lost its fiery strength, although there was not much relief in its breath, but the darkness brought its own relief from glaring sunlight, and Slade lit a small brown cigar and relaxed in his seat, breathing deeply and enjoying his peacefulness. Later he went to the saloon for a drink, had a couple of beers, then returned to the hotel to sleep. At sun-up he was awake and preparing to ride on, intent upon making end of track, now twenty-five miles out of Las Corros, before the end of the working day.

He spent the day in the saddle, tortured by the blazing sun and the tough terrain, but he followed the twin steel rails that led on and on across burning plain. It was the middle of the afternoon when he topped a rise beside the track and saw the construction camp spread out below him. Tracks were being laid at an astonishing rate, and black smoke curled skywards from the engine pushing the flat cars containing the ties and rails being used. There were tents in one area, where the men slept, and coaches on the track farther back from where the work was taking place. Well over to the left two large brown tents had been erected, and Slade narrowed his eyes as he studied them, for these would be the reason for his visit. A number of smaller tents had been erected beyond the two large ones, and he figured they contained the girls who had accompanied the mobile saloons.

He rode down the slope and entered the camp, making for Chain Becker's office, a rail car on a small loop-line that had been put in for convenience. Dismounting, Slade trailed his reins and climbed the steps of the car, ducking his head as he entered, and he took off his hat when he saw that Becker himself was not present. The clerk, busy at a desk, looked up, and got to his feet immediately.

'Howdy, Slade?' he greeted in nasal tones. He was tall and thin, dressed in a dark suit that looked as if it had been slept in continuously for six months. 'We got a wire telling us to expect you. Figured you would come out on the daily train.'

'Where's Chain, Tom?'

'Up at the front. Some of the men are downing tools. They want more dough.'

'To spend in those two tented saloons, huh?' Slade smiled grimly. It was a familiar story.

'That's right. We got a couple of troublemakers on the job, and when Chain can locate them he'll have them eating dust for what they're doing to our schedule.'

'These men know they won't draw full pay until the line reaches Jules Crossing,' Slade mused. 'Who is operating those saloons, Tom?'

'A smart faced jigger by the name of Flash Dan Delmont. We ain't ever come across him before, Slade. But he's real smooth and tricky. Watch out for him. He's got several fast guns working for him.'

'I'll go talk to Chain,' Slade said. 'See you later.'

He left the coach and remounted, riding on alongside the rails towards end of track, passing men who were coming away from the work area at the end of track. When he reached the end of the line he saw a small crowd gathered in a tight bunch around a couple of men who had stripped to the waist and were fist fighting.

Dismounting, Slade shouldered his way through the shouting men, until he reached the forefront of the circle formed about two men, and he saw that Becker was one of the fighters. Becker was a heavy, tall man, his massive body rippling with solid muscle, but he appeared to be getting the worst of the fight with a man even taller and heavier. Slade watched for a moment, his eyes narrowed, judging the situation, and his lips pulled tight for he saw that there was a wound in Becker's chest, just below the right shoulder, streaming blood, and lying in the dust nearby was a long-bladed knife.

Slade looked at the intent faces of the men forming the circle, knowing some of them by sight. But he saw a couple he did not know, and the expressions on them warned that these two had more than a passing interest in the outcome of the struggle. They were both wearing gunbelts, and a frown touched Slade's forehead when he saw the arms because the workers never carried guns.

34

Becker suddenly staggered under two jolting blows and then slipped down on one knee. The big construction camp boss was gasping for breath, his face and chest shining with sweat. He had an expression of desperation on his face, and blood was streaming from the wound in his chest. His large opponent kicked out heavily, catching Becker in the face, and as the camp boss went sprawling, the other man spun and snatched up the knife out of the dust.

Slade sprang forward, his sixshooter leaping into his hand, and as the big man bent to slash at the fallen Becker, Slade struck swiftly with the long barrel of his weapon, catching the man's wrist. There was a loud, agonized cry, and the knife went spinning back into the dust. Slade straightened, holstering his gun once more, and he kept an eye on the two watchers on the far side of the circle.

'What the hell?' The big man's face contorted in fury as he clutched his wrist and stared at Slade.

Across the circle the two men Slade was watching began to come forward, hands moving towards their holstered guns. They eased apart as they came, and Slade called sharply to them.

'Hold it, you two. If you're looking for trouble then stand where you are and declare yourselves.'

There was a hasty activity as the circle of railroaders scrambled to get out of the line of fire, and within scant seconds Slade was standing alone facing the three men, with Chain Becker stretched out at his feet. Both gunmen had halted, and now they studied Slade intently.

'Who in hell are you?' one of them demanded. 'What right you got to bust into a private fight?'

'I'm paid to bust up fights, private or otherwise, that take place on railroad land,' Slade retorted. 'Who are you? I take it you're connected with those tented saloons over there.'

'That's so,' came the steady reply. 'You a troubleshooter for the railroad.'

'Right. The name is Slade Hollister.'

'There's nothing you can do about us. Our saloons ain't on railroad land.'

'Mebbe not, but you two are on railroad land right now, so turn around and get out of here.' Slade turned his attention to the big man still clasping his bruised wrist. 'What about you, hombre?' he demanded. 'What's the fight about?'

'Becker figured to put me off the camp,' came the sullen reply. 'I was only telling the rest of the men they had to stick together for their rights.'

'Well I'm doing the telling now, and you are finished around here,' Slade said quietly. 'Get your time from the office and pull out. If I see your face inside camp limits in an hour from now I'll change its outline some.'

The man looked as if he would argue, but he shrugged his heavy shoulders and turned to pick up his shirt. He stalked away in the direction of the tents where the workers slept, and Slade kept his attention on the two gunmen.

'I told you this is private property,' he snapped. 'You're tres-passing. The warning I gave that big hombre also applies to you, and I don't mean maybe. Get out of here.'

'You put us out,' came the grim reply. 'There are two of us, and we've been waiting for you to show up, Troubleshooter.'

Slade tensed, knowing all the signs when he saw them. He wondered remotely if the trouble here had been engineered to get him or his father to the scene for some kind of showdown, and on top of the ambush in Big Bend by Drogo Rolph's gang, it looked as if someone was really anxious to rid the scene of the Hollisters.

'That suits me fine,' Slade responded harshly, and the next moment he was pulling his gun fast and smoothly, for both gunnies were reaching to their hips.

CHAPTER FIVE

Slade cleared leather smoothly, his gun muzzle tilting, his slitted gaze taking both men confronting him. He saw that the one on the right was ahead of the other in drawing, and concentrated upon him, cocking his hammer with a big thumb. He fired swiftly, teeth clenched at the angry blast. Dust flew from the man's shirt at the impact of the bullet, and Slade was already shifting his point of aim to cover the second man before the first could show any reaction. But the second man, witnessing the speed of Slade's draw, thrust his weapon deep into its holster instead of finishing his play, and lifted his hands in token of surrender as Slade's trigger finger teetered on the brink of squeezing.

'Hold it,' the man rapped. 'I want no part of it.'

The first man was sagging to the ground, and there was a growing spread of blood on his shirt front.

'Okay, get rid of your gunbelt,' ordered Slade. The cowed gunman unbuckled his belt and dropped it hastily. 'Now get your pard out of here, and if you are around this camp in an hour I'll come looking for you.'

The man bent and seized hold of his pard, half carrying, half dragging him away, and Slade watched him for a moment, then turned his attention to Chain Becker, who was pushing himself into a sitting position. The construction camp boss grinned tightly as he met Slade's hard gaze.

'I'm sure glad to see you, Slade,' he said.

'Looks like you were having rather more trouble than you could handle,' Slade replied, reaching down and pulling the man to his feet. 'Are you hurt bad?'

'Cal Bland touched me with his knife, but it ain't deep, and I figure I'll live. You're gonna have your hands full when you try to get rid of those tented saloons over there.'

'Can you handle the men in camp?' Slade demanded.

'I reckon so, now you've put Bland agoing, if he leaves, that is. He's been stirring up trouble for some time, and I only got

37

wise to him today. When I challenged him he pulled a knife on me, and I near cashed in my chips.'

'That's when I stepped in,' Slade said. He looked at the camp boss with intent gaze. 'You look like you got stomped by a mule, Chain.'

'It'll heal. But what about this Flash Dan Delmont?'

'I never heard of him before. He's never bothered any camp I've been around. Where did he come from?'

'He worked some of the other railroad camps, the bigger ones. I guess they all got too tough for him so he's come down to smaller fry, meaning us.'

'And he won't find us any easier to handle,' Slade said. 'I'll go over there and have a talk with him.'

They walked towards the office, and a number of the workers were still standing around in the background, having witnessed the end of the fight and the gunfight. Becker walked steadily, slightly favouring his wound, and when they reached the engine he signalled for the driver to call the workers together with the whistle. A series of shrill blasts tore apart the silence and sent strident echoes to the horizon.

Slade climbed onto the footplate of the engine, then gained the tender, and he faced the growing crowd of men who came reluctantly from the tents. Over a hundred men finally stood in the open before the engine, and they were silent and sullen, most of them looking down at the ground instead of at the faces of the two men who controlled them.

'Listen to me,' Slade said in ringing tones, his hands on his hips. 'I got no rights to tear down those tented saloons over there, but I guess you all know me well enough to know what my job is. In case any of you don't know, or have forgotten, then I'll remind you. I'm the chief troubleshooter for the railroad company. That means I get paid to take care of any trouble that comes up, if it's here in a camp or a gang of train robbers. Right now there is trouble here and I've come to put an end to it. Those two tented saloons over there are out of bounds to all workers in this camp. Can you hear me at the back there?' He paused and looked down at the upturned faces. I'll be across there tonight, and if I catch any man from this camp in either of those two tents I'll kick him from here to Las Corros and back, and he won't be working for this railroad company, or any other.'

Slade glanced at Becker, who was pale beneath his weathered exterior.

'I got a few things to say,' Chain Becker shouted angrily. 'Crowley, Scully, Beddoes and Willison, you men are through working for this railroad. Get your gear together, collect your pay, and get out. If I see anyone talking to you before you quit this camp the same will go for them. The rest of you can return to work at once. There's a couple of hours left yet for us to make up some of the time we lost today.'

Slade watched the men as they turned away. Most of them were keen to get to work, and had been intimidated by the troublemakers. With the removal of those troublemakers the work would go on easily.

'Thanks, Slade,' Becker said. 'Let's get over to the office so I can pay off those troublemakers. I want you to get a good look at them so you'll know them again. But they better not come within a mile of any camp I'm running. If I ever set eyes on them again I'll pull a gun.'

'You'd better let me take a look at the wound you collected, Chain,' Slade said. 'It could turn bad on you.'

'Yeah. Let's go into my compartment, huh? I could do with a slug of the hard stuff to bring me round a bit. It's been a tough week. But I heard what you and Hard Sam did to Rolph's outfit when they hit that train a few days ago. I figured you was too busy to spare me any attention.'

'I came soon as I got the word,' Slade said. 'Have you heard that Sam has been pulled out of the job? I'm sitting the big saddle now. Sam is taking over as Area Manager north of here.'

'I heard about it, and what you did here today proves you are more than a chip off the old block, Slade. I was real glad to see you here. But there's more to this trouble than Flash Dan Delmont and a couple of tented saloons, you know.'

'Frank Burden said something about trouble, but he didn't go into it. I figured to learn about it first-hand. That's always the best way, huh?' Slade spoke lightly as they entered the private compartment of the coach.

'This spur will be in Jules Crossing in a couple of months

39

now, Slade.' Becker opened a cupboard and produced a bottle of whisky and a couple of glasses, and poured two stiff drinks, handing one to Slade. 'When they open this line they're gonna put a freight company out of business. Harvey Trimble owns the Overland Freight Company, and Trimble is a tough man in Jules Crossing. I suspect that some of the men causing the trouble around here were put in by Trimble. If that is the case then there's a lot more trouble to come from that source.'

'I agree with you,' Slade said. 'What about Delmont? Is he in here for himself, or has he been put up to this?'

'I figure Delmont is the only one who can put you right on that, but he's a smooth character, Slade, and a tough one. Don't let his appearance fool you.' Becker pulled off his shirt and sat down, and Slade went to his side to examine the knife wound.

'It doesn't look serious, but I figure you've got to take care of it, Chain,' Slade commented. 'I guess we could do worse than waste a little of your good whisky, huh?' He took up the bottle, pulled the stopper and poured a quantity of the liquor into the wound. Becker cursed mildly through clenched teeth.

'You're the hell of a doctor, Slade!' he complained. 'I reckon I better get back out there and make sure those knotheads keep at it until sundown. If I can't break their hearts then I'll surely break their backs.'

'I'll take a ride over to see Delmont,' Slade said.

'You better watch your step over there,' Becker warned. 'I don't figure Flash Dan Delmont is any pushover.'

'If I start pushing he'll go four ways from the middle,' Slade promised.

They left the coach and Becker went forward to where the work was again in progress. Slade stared after the camp boss for a moment, then swung into his saddle and let the horse pick its way around the heaps of equipment. He rode over to the nearest of the two tents and dismounted, aware that he was under scrutiny. He moved forward, pausing to look at the glaringly painted sign hanging over the gaping doorway to the tent. It bore the legend FLASH DAN'S in gold lettering.

Slade had seen the inside of such establishments before, had sided Hard Sam in several operations that ended the activities of men like Flash Dan Delmont who had tried to make fortunes out of hard working railroaders. But this place was more lavish than any he had seen.

There was a man seated at the piano, tinkling idly on the keys, and the music sounded out of place in this wilderness. A tender was behind the bar, polishing glasses, and a tall, well dressed man, looking something like a gambler, was on this side of the bar, talking to him. There was no sign of strong-arm men, and Slade smiled thinly as he went to where the two men were standing, because he was certain the bully boys were within calling distance.

'Where's Delmont?' he demanded harshly when he reached the two men, and the tender looked up swiftly, as if startled. Slade figured he had been under observation from the moment he left the construction camp, but he remained expressionless, his hands at his sides.

The gambler turned to face him, and for a moment they studied one another. Slade saw a tall, elegantly dressed man in a black broadcloth suit. He was wearing a high collar and a black string tie. His waistcoat was of red silk, and a fancy watchchain decorated the front of it. The handsome face was smooth, expressionless, and the brown eyes were hard and inscrutable as they studied Slade.

'You're Delmont,' Slade said, nodding. 'You look like the kind of man who would run a place like this.'

'I'm Flash Dan. And you're Slade Hollister, Chief Troubleshooter for Middle and Far Western.'

'I've got news for you, Delmont. As of now you're wasting your time. I don't have any authority to pull this tent down around your fancy ears, but I do control the men out there working on the railroad, and they've been given their orders. Not one of them will set foot in either of these tents tonight or any other night, so you might as well close down, pack up and get out.'

'I've heard a lot about you, Hollister,' Delmont answered, and there was much in his tone to suggest that he had not even listened to Slade's warning. 'But there's nothing you can do about this place. It ain't on your right of way. If your men want to visit us when they've done their day's work then it's up to them.'

'It's against the rules of the job,' Slade said. 'They get their week-ends free, and they're at liberty to go into Las Corros for their pleasure, but during the week they don't carouse or gamble. They have to be up at the crack of dawn, and by the time the sun is shining they're hard at it. They don't look for pleasures during the week. Take heed of this warning you're getting, Delmont. If there is any trouble around here I'll know where to come.'

'I'll be looking for you,' Delmont said with a grin. 'How about a drink on the house before you go?'

'I'd rather be shot than poisoned,' Slade said tightly. 'The slop you push across this bar would burn the paint off a red-skin's hide.'

'It makes your men work all the harder,' Delmont said.

Slade shook his head and turned away. He saw a couple of hardcases standing in the doorway, but they made no move towards him as he departed, and he did not look back as he swung into his saddle and rode into the camp once more.

Later he ate supper with Chain Becker, and the sun was gone by the time they left the coach to have a smoke. Stars glimmered in the velvet sky. The breeze was cool, scented with intangible aromas it had picked up on its long trip across hundreds of miles of mountain, forest and desert. It was a time for feeling peaceful and relaxed, but Slade was on edge because he knew a showdown was imminent. He had to make a move, and it would cost him a lot if it turned out to be a wrong one.

'Some of the men are slinking across to Delmont's,' Becker said presently.

'I see 'em,' Slade retorted.

'I'm short-handed now,' Becker went on. 'I can't afford to lose any more men. I can't fire any you find in those tents, Slade.'

'I reckon that too. So why don't you gather a dozen men you can trust, Chain? Send them into Delmont's and let them start a ruckus. They can take pick handles with them, a couple of axes, huh? If someone is caught cheating at cards it would be a normal thing for a man to put an axe through the roulette wheel.'

'Now you're talking!' Eagerness touched Becker's tones. 'I got just the crew for that sort of thing. I'll call 'em out and take 'em on over.'

'Give it another hour or so,' Slade said. 'I want to take a ride around the camp and see what kind of animals we got waiting out there in the night. Let your men go into the saloons, Chain, but don't start anything until I show up there. Okay?'

'It's your show,' Becker replied. 'We'll back your play.'

Slade nodded and departed, fetching his horse and saddling up. He rode out of camp, aware of men sneaking across to one or the other of the tented saloons. But he had other things on his mind, and when he began to circle the camp he moved slowly and steadily, using his ears as well as his eyes. He had covered more than half the perimeter when he topped a rise and spotted a fire in the cover of a distant gully. He rode in closer, then dismounted before he could be heard and closed in on foot.

There was a camp in the gully, with all the troublemakers Becker had fired lounging in it. Big Cal Bland was there, sitting before the fire, staring balefully into the leaping flames, his face ruddy in the uncertain light, his eyes glinting as he mused over his particular problems. Slade lay flat in cover and watched, listening intently, hoping to learn something from the conversation going on, but it was obvious that no one dared speak to Bland, and the others kept glancing in the big man's direction while they spoke amongst themselves. Slade was preparing to move away when Cal Bland got to his feet and turned to the others.

'Okay,' he said. 'I've decided. We don't wait any longer. We're going to start destroying railroad property. There's plenty of dynamite. Foley, you can handle that stuff. You get as much of it as you want, take a couple of good men, and go back along the line to blow up the trestle bridges they built. I figure a shrewd blow now will cost the railroad valuable time, and we've got to block the completion of the line into Jules Crossing until Trimble's overland freight contracts are renewed. You got that?'

'What about Hollister?' someone demanded uneasily.

'He's a man, that's all,' Bland said. 'I'd prove it to you if I could get my hands on him.'

'He's no fool. He wouldn't let you within arm's length of him, Cal. He's a gunhand, and one of the fastest. I've seen him in action before and he's no slouch.'

'Yeah,' Bland said heavily. 'All these years we had Hard

Sam to face, and now he's hauling his freight out of the business there's his boy, just as big and dangerous. I figure we got to do something about Slade Hollister before we can go ahead with our business. You guys stay put while I go in to talk to Delmont. I won't be gone long.' Bland peered around for a few moments, as if daring anyone to object. Then he stalked away out of the circle of firelight. His voice floated back through the shadows. 'Don't anybody get any fancy ideas about pulling out. I'm running this show and if anyone steps out of line and causes us more trouble than we already got then I'll break his back for him.'

There was no reply, and moments later Slade heard hoofs pounding away on the hard ground nearby. He eased away from the gully, collected his horse and rode back to camp. He turned the animal into the rope corral, hitched up his gunbelt and moved through the shadows towards the tented saloons.

There were music and voices sounding from inside the two tents, and Slade did not press close for there were hardcases standing in the doorways, obviously on the watch for him. He went around the back of the tents, finding more guards, and stood watching their dark figures for a moment, considering his next move, and he knew he had to do something decisive, although he was badly outnumbered. He sat down in the shadows and watched the rear of the tents, until he remembered the greatest hazard to a tent was fire. He smiled tightly in the darkness, then began to move in slowly, crawling steadily, stalking the guard on watch at the rear.

When he arose he was only a few feet from the nearest man, and his gun barrel slammed hard against the guard's skull. Holstering the gun, Slade dragged the man clear, then went close to the back of the tent. He could hear muted sounds coming through from the interior, and he began to pull handfuls of dried buffalo grass to pile against the tinder-dry canvas. When he had a large heap he struck a match and ignited it.

He was not prepared for what happened next. The flames licked greedily at the taut canvas, and suddenly the whole rear of the tent exploded into roaring flame. Slade staggered backwards, quickly losing himself in the surrounding shadows, and he heard screams and startled yells as the danger became ap-

44

parent to those inside the tent. Men and saloon girls began rushing outside to safety.

Moving around the tent, Slade took up a position many yards clear in front. He stood watching the tent become engulfed with voracious flame, and fleeing figures were pouring out through the doorway, shouting and yelling.

Returning to Becker's coach, Slade entered, well pleased with what he had accomplished. He found the clerk getting up from the telegraph equipment, a message pad in his hands, and Slade frowned when he caught a glimpse of the man's pallid face.

'What is it?' he demanded. 'Something wrong?'

'I'll say there is,' the clerk replied, holding out the pad. 'This message just came through for you, Slade. It's about San Blanca. Drogo Rolph showed up there as expected, and Jim Longley was waiting for him. The trouble is, Longley wasn't good enough to handle Rolph, who got away, and Jim Longley is dead.'

CHAPTER SIX

Slade stood stunned for long moments, staring at the grim message on the pad, and there was a picture of Jim Longley in his mind. The door of the coach opened and Becker appeared, his face black but beaming.

'Hey, Slade, you missed something out there,' the camp boss said joyfully. 'Flash Dan is burning out of existence. We didn't have to lift a finger to do anything. Him and his hardcases are trying to save what they can, but it's a hopeless job.' He paused, taking in Slade's expression. 'Say, what's wrong?' he demanded.

The clerk told him, and Becker began to curse. Slade dragged his mind clear of the hard thoughts hitting him and took a swift breath.

'You've got a train going back to Las Corros tonight, Chain?' he demanded.

'Sure. You wanta ride it?'

'I'd better get back to Big Bend soon as I can. And there's something you've got to know, Chain.' Slade explained about overhearing Cal Bland's talk around the campfire in the gully. 'You better double your guards on the explosives store and watch out for trouble. Tell your men to shoot any of those hombres you fired today if they show up around here. They're tied in with the Overland Freight Company. I'll be back this way soon as I can and we'll see what can be done about your troubles. But with Delmont out of it most of your present worries will be over.'

'If any of those hombres try to start anything around here they will get the surprise of their lives,' Becker said sharply. 'I made plans for such events, Slade, and we're fully covered all ways to the middle.'

'Good. What time does your train leave?' Slade was impatient to be on his way.

'In thirty minutes. It'll drop you in Las Corros come two am. It will enable you to connect with the train for Big

46

Bend. You could be at Area Headquarters come sun-up.'

'Fine. That will do me. I'll send Harry Kelleher on here to you, Chain. He's a good man. He'll be able to handle this.'

'Fine. But before you leave you could have a visitor. Flash Dan will suspect you of knowing something about the fire that burned him out of business.'

'If he comes probing around here he'll find he's got more on his plate than he can eat,' Slade said sharply.

But the train pulled out before Delmont was finished around the smouldering ruins of his tents, and Slade was aboard, his blankets in a box car, and he slept fitfully until they pulled into Las Corros.

The sun was low in the eastern sky when Slade stepped off the train at Big Bend, and the first person he saw was Frank Burden on the platform. The Area Manager looked as if he hadn't slept all night, and he started towards Slade when he saw him.

'Where in hell have you been?' Burden demanded. 'Don't you know you've lost Jim Longley?'

Slade halted in midstride, and his teeth gleamed in a mirthless grin as he stared at the older man.

'Frank,' he said quietly, 'I've already had about as much as I can stomach from you. Now put up or shut up. Stick to your job and leave me to attend to mine. Sure I know about Longley. I was at end of track on the Jules Crossing spur when I heard about it. What the hell do you figure I was doing, anyway? I'm on the job and I'm doing my best.'

Burden's eyes were bloodshot. He stared at Slade, his teeth clenched, his fists knotted.

'Lola went through to Las Corros last night,' he said. 'She went to meet you, Slade. Don't try to deny it.'

'I left end of track after midnight,' Slade said tightly. 'You can check it out. I burned out Delmont's tents and he'll quit. I've learned that the Overland Freight Company is causing the trouble Chain Becker is getting, and we can wire that information to the marshal in Jules Crossing. A man named Cal Bland is bossing the gang causing us all the trouble. He's planning on stealing dynamite and blowing up all the trestle bridges between Las Corros and end of track. Now you get to work and figure out what to do to stop him. Get the law on it. And,

47

Frank,' Slade paused, his voice dry, his tones level and unemotional. 'If you ever accuse me again of meeting your wife, of seeing her on the quiet, I'll tear you limb from limb with my teeth. Do I make myself clear?'

Burden opened his mouth to speak, but Slade turned away, his blanket roll under his arm. He left the depot and went across to his home, finding Hard Sam awake and cooking breakfast in the kitchen.

'Hell, I'm glad to see you,' Sam said. 'You look like hell, son. I guess you've heard about San Blanca, huh?'

'I got word.' Slade sat down.

'It ain't a pretty tale,' Hard Sam rasped, throwing more bacon into the big pan. 'Harry Kelleher wired me – he doesn't know yet you've taken over – and said when he got to San Blanca Longley was dead, gunned down, and Drogo Rolph long gone. I called Harry back, and he should be arriving sometime today.'

'I should have gone on to San Blanca myself,' Slade said in hard tones. 'I had that gal, Maisie Clapham. I could have travelled with her and used her as bait to lure Rolph out into the open. I would have nailed him.'

'Slade, you got to accept that you ain't able to be in two places at once, and you did a good job at end of track. I got a wire an hour ago saying that Delmont and his outfit pulled out of their site in the middle of the night with what little they could salvage. Did you burn him out?'

'Yeah. But there's one more thing you should know, Sam.' Slade spoke through his teeth, his eyes glittering. He related his encounter with Frank Burden. 'I can't take much more of his attitude. If he accuses me once more of running after his wife I'll put a stop to him.'

'Hold up, Slade, and think about it,' Hard Sam said sharply. 'Frank Burden is a good man, and you can't blame him for acting the way he does. I figure that Lola gal will up and leave him someday, anyhow, and good riddance. Bear with Frank, Slade. He deserves a lot of sympathy. He's an old man gone to pieces over a younger woman, and there ain't a more sorrier looking sight than Frank Burden these days.'

'Okay. But maybe you better have a word with him, tell him to lay off. I got an idea it's Brady who's seeing Lola.'

'You got any proof to that?' Sam's face was inscrutable, but his pale eyes were glittering as he looked into Slade's set features.

'No. If I had I'd do something. It's getting so Frank ain't gonna be responsible for his actions. Did you get a look at Ned Bunch yesterday when he was brought in?'

'Yeah.' Sam turned out the contents of the big fry-pan onto their plates, then fetched the coffee pot and sat down. 'What gives there, Slade? How come you got a man like Bunch laying for you?'

'I wish I knew.' Slade shook his head as he began to eat. 'I don't know why none of Rolph's old gang was with him on that raid we foiled, Sam. Something is going on we ain't heard about yet. I was talking to Lola when I got back with that gold. She wants to get shot of Burden. That much she made plain. I got the feeling she's hinting to Burden that I am the man she's seeing on the quiet. I figure she hopes Burden will blow his top and come for me and that I'll kill him. On top of that, when I bought Brady a drink the other day he hinted that Drogo Rolph must be getting information about which trains to rob. If you think about it, he never seems to pick a wrong one.'

There was a knock at the door and Sam got up to answer. Slade finished his coffee and leaned back in his seat, his mind fully occupied with his problems. When Sam returned he was holding a wire, reading it over and over again.

'What is it, Sam?' Slade demanded.

'It's for you, from Brady,' Sam retorted. 'Says he's on his way to San Blanca on the dawn freight, that he got a tip-off Rolph is gonna hit the express car of the eight-fifteen through San Blanca.'

'Is there anything in that express car worth taking, Sam?' Slade demanded.

'Yeah. I got the word last evening,' Sam said reluctantly. 'I've been standing in for you while you've been at end of track. There's a special shipment of bullion on the eight-fifteen through San Blanca.'

'How much?' Slade pressed.

'One hundred thousand dollars worth.' Sam shook his head. 'And there ain't a damn thing we can do about it now.'

'Wire San Blanca,' Slade said instantly. 'Harry Kelleher is

still there. If he boards the train at least it will have some protection.'

'I'll attend to it right away,' Sam said, making for the door. 'It'll be close, but if Harry is standing by, like I know he always does, we should be able to get him to board that train. Brady will meet it at Apache Well. It means Harry will be on his own for three hours. Give me a couple of minutes, Slade. I'll be back presently. I'd better go set the wheels in motion. Burden will be over there, and the less you see of him the better, huh?'

'You can say that again,' Slade said angrily. He drank another cup of coffee as he considered, then got up and went through to the parlour, studying the map on the wall that had been there for as long as he could remember. It showed the railroad area that was now his Division, and ran his eye along the rail routes, picking out San Blanca, Apache Well, and Jules Crossing. Brady was on his way to Apache Well, where he would meet the eight-fifteen through San Blanca. It would reach Apache Well around ten-thirty. But what was Brady doing, going to Apache Well without first reporting in? The wire which had just arrived gave the information of the tip-off about Rolph's latest raid too late for anything constructive to be done about it. When had Phil Brady left town?

It came to Slade then that Lola Burden had gone to Las Corros the night before, so Frank Burden had told him. Had she gone to meet Brady? Was that why Brady had been in that area? Slade recalled his suspicions that Brady was the man Lola was fooling around with, and a heavy sigh escaped him as he tried to sort out the facts in his mind. He didn't need these nagging side issues on top of Drogo Rolph.

Sam returned, and Slade found his father hard faced and boiling with suppressed anger.

'I can understand why you're getting to the end of your rope with Frank Burden,' Hard Sam said. 'I came near to hitting him myself. He's like a madman this morning, Slade, and you better stay well clear of him. This news about the bullion on the San Blanca eight-fifteen is sending him up the wall in three different directions. He's the Area Manager, and this shipment is coming through his area without his knowledge.'

'Is that a fact?' Slade shook his head slowly. 'How come? You got word of it okay last night, you said.'

'That I did.' There was a grim note in Sam's harsh tones. 'I wonder if someone higher up is getting the same idea Brady gave to you.'

'About someone in the know passing on vital information about the money shipments to Rolph?' Slade nodded slowly. 'I figure we should have thought of that before Brady did, Sam.'

'We've got to start by suspecting someone,' Sam declared. 'I tell you one thing, Slade, and that ain't maybe. Brady is right about someone passing information to the gang. If you figure how many trains Rolph has hit, and how many times he took the right one, well, no man could be that lucky without some help.

'How many men are in that position of trust in our area?' Slade demanded. 'How many know in advance about our gold and money shipments? Can we get a list and work on it?'

'Look, you're gonna have your work cut out getting after Rolph, and you'd better start right now. I'm sticking around here for a few days regardless of my orders, and I'll find out who had knowledge of those shipments that were lifted by Rolph. I figure we could lay some kind of a trap for the informer, Slade. It won't be easy to uncover him, and it will take time, but leave it to me.'

'Be glad to,' Slade said instantly. 'I'm quite happy to go and shoot it out with the gang, but all this high-powered thinking sticks in my craw. What do you figure my best move would be now?'

'Nothing until word comes through about the San Blanca eight-fifteen,' Sam replied, shaking his head.

Sam departed to start making his discreet inquiries into the men who had knowledge of the movement of gold and money on the railroad, and Slade cleaned up, changing his dusty clothes, washing and shaving, and his thoughts were fast moving and furious. He started going through the names of the men he knew would have knowledge of the contents carried in the express cars, but he could not say with any degree of certainty which men were likely to be in the pay of Drogo Rolph.

Then he let his thoughts return to Phil Brady, and for a long time he considered all the aspects about Brady. The man had contacts amongst the lawless element that lived on the fringe of the railroad – petty thieves, pickpockets, gamblers who travelled the rail routes cheating the passengers. But then every good troubleshooter had his own lines to information, and he knew Brady was no exception. But there was something in the background of Brady's life that showed at times in the man's manner, when he could not quite hide his feelings and emotions, and Slade had considered the fact many times. Now he wondered at it, and tried to imagine Phil Brady as the renegade employee feeding the vital information to the gang.

Sam returned later, and his face was grim. Slade made coffee while his father talked.

'I made some inquiries with the help of Colonel Bill's office,' Sam said harshly. 'There are about half a dozen employees who would know about the movement of pay trains and bullion shipments, apart from the men who load and unload, but they would only learn about it on the day the stuff was being moved. Our man is one of half a dozen who would know about it days in advance, and you know what, Slade? Frank Burden is one of them, and Phil Brady.'

'Burden might be a number of unpleasant things these days,' Slade said, 'but he wouldn't turn renegade, Sam. I'd stake my life on that. Yet there's this trouble he's having with Lola! I don't understand a lot of things. Lola wants Frank out of this area. Why? Has she discovered that he's in league with the outlaws, passing on the information? Is that why she wants him moved, so he can't contact Rolph any more?'

'And Brady. But he wouldn't know about all the shipments, only those he's ordered to guard,' Sam said. 'This is a tough one all right, Slade, but I figure there is one way to beat this racket.'

'I'll be interested to hear it,' Slade said promptly.

'I've made a list of these men who are in the know in advance,' Sam paused and thought for a moment. 'Now I reckon if I take them one at a time and seep through information individually about a non-existent gold shipment, the one who has the information when Rolph's gang strikes must be our man.'

Slade's eyes glistened for a moment, and then he shook his head doubtfully. 'We'd be taking a number of unknown factors on trust in a case like that,' he said. 'Coincidence for one.'

'You got a better idea of eliminating the innocent?' Sam asked.

'No.' Slade grinned mirthlessly. 'You go ahead with your idea, Sam. It could pay off, and we sure need a break now. I'm going back to end of track. There are some hardcases around there need cleaning out, and Harvey Trimble, who owns the Overland Freight Company, has got to be talked to. He's sent some the hardcases in to cause trouble for the railroad. But I want to have another talk with Lola. Burden said she went to Las Corros last night, and Brady had to be in that area if he went on to Apache Well this morning. I want some straight talking with Lola.'

'Better watch out that word of your meeting her don't get back to Burden,' Sam warned. 'He's working himself into a killing mood again over Lola.'

'This is railroad business,' Slade said harshly. 'You can contact me at Las Corros. I'll jump the eleven o'clock freight. Then I'll have to wait for the work train to end of track, so I'll be around Las Corros for a spell.'

'Okay, and as soon as anything comes through from Brady or Kelleher I'll wire you,' Sam said. 'Good hunting, Slade.'

Slade nodded and prepared to depart. He was not in an optimistic frame of mind, but his determination made up for any doubts which he had. He boarded the freight train heading for Las Corros, aware that Frank Burden watched him leaving, and during the long trip he wore his brain to a frazzle trying to reason out who could be at the back of the information leak, and why.

Las Corros was baking in the hot afternoon sun when Slade dropped off the freight and went to the telegraph office. The operator nodded at sight of him and turned to pick up a message pad. He had a grim expression on his face as he handed it to Slade. Rolph had hit the San Blanca eight-fifteen at a place called Sourdough Creek. The entire shipment of gold had been stolen, and Harry Kelleher was dead, gunned down in the uneven fight he had waged against the gang. Phil Brady had not joined the train at Apache Well. Kelleher had been alone.

CHAPTER SEVEN

For long moments Slade stood frozen with the message pad in his trembling hand. Then he looked up to find the telegraphist staring at him, and he fought for his composure.

'Did Brady stop off here last night?' he demanded.

'Sure,' the man said. 'He got in off the freight from Big Bend around two in the morning.'

'Is Lola Burden in town? I heard she came up from Big Bend yesterday.'

'Sure. She arrived. But I don't know if she stayed. I heard her talking to Hank Billings on the platform as I passed them, and she mentioned something about El Paso.'

'Okay, thanks. I'll be around here until the work train pulls out for end of track. Got any idea when that'll be today?'

'Six this evening. You got a few hours to spare.'

'Don't let them leave without me,' Slade said. 'And if any urgent messages come through for me then send someone to look for me. I got some inquiries to make around town.'

'Leave it to me,' the telegraphist assured him.

Slade tore the flimsy from the pad and folded it, putting it into a breast pocket, and he went out to the street, pausing to look around in the brilliant sunlight. His lips were a firm line in his face, his eyes narrowed and glittering balefully. As he walked along the street to the only hotel that Las Corros boasted, Slade again wondered about Phil Brady. He had certainly sent the information about the train being robbed, but it had arrived too late for anything to be done about it, except get Harry Kelleher on the train and eventually killed.

Entering the hotel, Slade asked the clerk for Lola Burden, and learned she was in her room. Slade took a deep breath, mounted the stairs and knocked at Lola's door. She answered immediately, as if she had been expecting him, but her beautiful face changed expression when she saw him.

'Expecting someone else, huh?' he inquired, pushing past her to enter the room.

'What do you want here?' she demanded angrily as he turned to face her. 'You've got no right to come busting in here, Slade.'

She was dressed in a long blue silk dressing gown which was open a long way down the front from the neck. She was barefoot, and Slade figured she had just got out of bed, until he saw that her face was carefully made up. Her dark eyes were smouldering with emotion, and he wondered if her anger was simulated. But she was obviously not pleased to see him, and he turned his attention from her and looked around the room. There was nowhere a man could hide, he saw instantly, and wondered if Phil Brady had been here.

'Frank is concerned about you being here,' he said.

'So? It's too bad if he doesn't like it when I've had my fill of Big Bend for a spell,' she retorted. 'That one-horse town makes me want to start peeling the wallpaper. I had to get out of there.'

'Who stayed with you last night?' he demanded sharply.

'Stayed with me?' Her face hardened its expression. 'You've got a nerve, Slade, coming here and asking questions like that. Unless you're jealous.' A smile played around her lips and her eyes brightened. She closed the door and came towards him, and he stretched out his left arm and fended her off, his knuckles pushing hard against her shoulder. She almost went off balance, and again her expression changed. 'Damn you, Slade,' she rapped in vicious tones. 'Who in hell do you think you are?'

'Frank knew I was in this area yesterday,' he retorted. 'He had the idea you came here to meet me. Did you put that idea into his head?'

'Seeing you here was the last thing in my mind,' she said, smiling again.

'I know that.' He was thinking swiftly. 'It's Brady now, huh? You saw Brady here last night. He was with you.'

Several different emotions chased across her lovely face, but her dark eyes were narrowed and calculating. She was wondering if he was making guesses, and it was obvious to his perceptive gaze. He took the flimsy from his pocket and unfolded it, watching her the whole time.

'Don't try to deny it, Lola,' he rasped. 'Brady was in Las

55

Corros last night. He sent us a message about another Drogo Rolph raid coming off, and he should have been on the northbound freight out of here in the early hours. He was supposed to have met the San Blanca eight-fifteen at Apache Well, but he didn't make it. Rolph hit that train at Sourdough Creek, and Harry Kelleher was killed.'

Her face changed expression again, and now shock filled her eyes. Her head shook slowly, as if she could not accept what he was saying. Slade watched her intently, his suspicions concerning Phil Brady in full flood. Had Brady got together with this woman in an attempt to get Frank Burden out of this Area? Slade felt his mind reeling under an assault of questions. He was wondering what to say next when there was a knock at the door, and before Lola could move the door opened. Phil Brady himself entered the room.

It was likely that both men were equally shocked by the presence of the other, but Slade quickly recovered. He took a swift breath as Brady stared open-mouthed at him.

'What the hell are you doing here, Phil?' Slade snapped.

Brady closed his mouth and gulped, then flung a swift glance at the silent woman. When he looked at Slade again some of his shock had receded.

'Why weren't you at Apache Well to meet the San Blanca eight-fifteen like you wired?' Slade rasped.

'I got into trouble here, before I could hop the northbound freight like I planned,' Brady said.

'Trouble? What kind of trouble?'

'I took a drink in the saloon, and when I left someone cracked me over the head with a pistol barrel. When I came to the freight had gone.'

'Why didn't you wire Big Bend that you couldn't make it?' he demanded. 'I would have made other arrangements for Harry Kelleher.'

'I wasn't in any condition to think straight,' Brady muttered. 'I was concussed. You can check with the Doc here if you don't want to take my word for it. Hell, why wouldn't I want to make that train? I got the tip-off about Rolph in the first place.'

'Kelleher was killed in the raid,' Slade flung at him. 'You weren't there to back him, and I wired him to expect you at Apache Well.'

'Rolph did hit that train?' Brady gasped.

'Didn't you think he would, after getting a tip-off?' Slade demanded.

'Where?' Brady's face was pale.

'Sourdough Creek.'

'What did they get away with?'

'One hundred thousand dollars in gold bars.'

Slade's keen eyes were taking in Brady's tough figure, and the man's dark eyes still seemed to be trying to conceal a secret. He looked at Brady's open neck – the man's shirt was unbuttoned almost to the waist, and his lips tightened when he saw tell-tale marks on the bronzed flesh. Striding forward, he reached out and grasped a handful of Brady's shirt, ripping it away from the man's body. There were bites in profusion on the muscular neck and shoulders, and Slade gritted his teeth.

'Just as I figured,' he said tightly. 'It wasn't a blow on the head that kept you off that train, Brady. It was Lola! You stayed with her last night instead of doing your duty, and if you had joined the San Blanca eight-fifteen at Apache Well Harry Kelleher might still be alive.'

'Damn you, Hollister.' Anger spilled into Brady's dark eyes. 'How come you figure everything to your own advantage? You reckon I want your job? Well to hell with you. I'm quitting here and now.'

He swung his right fist then, in a powerful blow intended to connect with Slade's jaw. Slade moved inside quickly, his left fist sledging up into the region of Brady's heart. The man gasped and sprawled away, but Slade followed him, letting go with a right that cracked solidly against Brady's jaw. Brady went down on one knee and Slade bent and grasped him, dragging him upright, his anger flaring, his control lost momentarily. He punished Brady with his heavy right fist, sledging it against the man's bronzed face, and Brady couldn't take it, sagging in Slade's grasp.

Lola was screaming, clawing at Slade from behind, her long nails raking his back and the left side of his face. He paused to half turn towards her, and he gave her a backhander that cracked against the side of her head, sending her half-way across the room to fall in a heap on the floor.

'I'll get around to you in a moment,' he rasped, and returned his attention to Brady, holding the man upright, peering animal-like into his battered face. 'Brady, you don't quit,' he said. 'I'll fire you when you can go. Right now you're gonna put me straight on several matters. I want to know where you got the tip-off from.'

'You know nobody ever opens up about their network of informers,' Brady said through his teeth. 'I'm not telling you, Slade. Okay, so you're mad about Kelleher getting his. So am I. But it wasn't my fault I didn't get there in time.'

Slade thrust the man away, and Brady fell to his knees. For a moment Slade stared down at him, holding his temper in check. Then he turned to the woman. Lola had sprawled to the floor, and she still crouched there, staring up at Slade with hate-filled eyes.

Hell hath no fury like a woman scorned, Slade thought as he crossed to her. His big hands reached for her shoulders and he dragged her roughly to her feet. There was a red mark high on her left cheekbone where the back of his hand had caught her, and he grinned when he saw it.

'Okay, Lola,' he said. 'You and me are gonna have just one more talk. It's none of my business who in hell you run around with, but stop hinting to Frank that it's me. If Frank comes to me just once more accusing me of seeing you I'll come after you and you'll get the worst roughing up you've ever had. Is that clear? I'm through playing games.'

She nodded silently and he let go of her, letting her fall again. Turning to Brady, who was watching him through narrowed eyes, he motioned for the man to get up.

'You and me have got some travelling to do, Phil,' he snapped. 'Let's get moving.'

Brady staggered to his feet and made for the door. Slade followed Brady down to the lobby, then out to the sidewalk, and there Brady turned to face him. Slade stood ready to continue the fight, but Brady obviously had other things on his mind.

'Slade, listen to me,' Brady said tightly. There were bruises turning out on his heavy face. 'I did everything right last night. But it wasn't my fault I got slugged.'

'I'll accept that, Phil,' Slade said harshly. 'But why didn't you notify the office at Big Bend when you missed the freight out? I would have put the local law onto the case. They would have had some deputies aboard the train when Rolph hit it. But you didn't think of that, huh? You were taken up with Lola.'

'What about that?' Brady demanded, fingering the red patches on his jawline. 'Didn't you go overboard for Lola some time ago?'

'A long time ago,' Slade retorted. 'That was before she married Burden. I ain't seen her since that day. Burden is in a killing mood. He's got me figured for the man fooling around with Lola, and I'm telling you here and now, Phil. If Burden does come for me because of Lola I'll tell him straight it's you.'

'What are we gonna do about Rolph?' Brady was keen to change the subject.

'Where did your tip-off come from?'

'I won't tell you that.' Brady set his teeth, his brown eyes glittering.

'Okay, but can you learn where Rolph is hiding out from this informant?'

'No. It's too dangerous for anyone to try and get hold of that information. What happens now?'

'You want to quit or go on with the job?' Slade's voice was smooth now.

'I'll go on with it if you're prepared to overlook what went on here,' Brady said.

'It's none of my business as far as Lola goes,' Slade said thoughtfully. 'But you've got to live with the knowledge that Harry Kelleher might have survived if you had done your duty properly last night.'

'I know I wasn't to blame in any way,' Brady retorted. 'I'll live with it, and one of these days we'll get our own back on Rolph and his bunch.'

'I hope you're right. We're going to Sourdough Creek. I want to pick up tracks of the gang and try once more to trail them to their hideout. I had some business at end of track, but that will have to wait now. Rolph is the most important job we got on our hands, and the sooner we nail him down tight the better.'

'What am I to do?' Brady asked.

'Go down to the depot and send wires to Big Bend and Sourdough Creek. Inform Hard Sam at Big Bend that we're on our way to track the gang. Tell him to hire a couple more men to replace Longley and Kelleher. He can reach us by telegraph at Sourdough Creek. I want horses waiting for us at the Creek. Attend to that, Phil. I got a couple of visits to make around here. Find out when we can get a train out of here.'

Brady nodded and departed. Slade started along the boards, making for the law office, and when he reached the building he found the town marshal sitting on a chair in the doorway.

'Howdy, Hart,' Slade said, and the lawman got to his feet, a tall, heavily built man in his forties. His green shirt was sweat stained and dusty, his face stubbled. 'Looks like you've been having a tough time of it. Anything wrong?'

'Nothing as bad as your spots of bother,' came the steady reply. 'Anything I can do for you?'

'Did you see Brady around town last night?'

'Yeah. Had a couple of hands of poker with him, as a matter of fact. Why?'

'Did he report getting slugged last night?'

'Yeah. It was after he left the saloon. He told me he had a train to catch.'

'Did you see him after the slugging?'

'Sure did. He staggered back into the saloon, blood running down his face. We carried him over to Doc's.'

'What kind of state was he in after the Doc looked him over?'

'Unsteady. Suffering concussion, I figure. The Doc told him to rest up for a couple of days, but Brady figured he had more important things to do.'

'What about Lola Burden?' Slade's face was expressionless as the marshal glanced sharply at him. 'Did you see her arrive from Big Bend?'

'Yep. I'm down at the depot watching all the trains go by. I like to know who's coming into or leaving my town.'

'What did she do after arriving?'

'Put up at the hotel, and I didn't see her any more.'

'Thanks, Hart.' Slade turned away. 'See you around.'

Slade walked back along the street, intending to go to the Doc's house, but he saw the medico coming along the sidewalk, black leather medical bag in one hand. They met in front of the hotel.

'Hello, Slade, how you keeping?' Doc Hollis asked. He was

short and fleshy, dressed in a crumpled brown store suit. His tie was crooked, his hat weatherbeaten and dusty.

'I'm fine, Doc, but you look like you been through a mill sideways. I was on my way to talk to you.'

'You're lucky you seen me. I just got in from the Peters' ranch and I'm on my way to the Silver Lode mine. A couple men been hurt in a rock fall.'

'I won't keep you a couple of minutes.' Slade glanced around the deserted street. 'You treated Phil Brady last night, Doc. How badly was he hurt?'

'Not bad at all. Someone tried to bend a gun barrel over his head, that's all. It gave him a headache, but after a good night's sleep he should have got up feeling fine.'

'What about last night? That's what I'm interested in. Would he have had a clear mind after the slugging? Would he have been able to remember everything he had to do?'

'That's hard to say. I did advise him to go to bed and get a good night's sleep. A blow like that can affect a man in different ways. He could have forgotten everything until this morning, or he might not have been affected at all.'

'Okay, Doc. Thanks for your time. See you around.'

Slade leaned a shoulder against a post and stared along the street. His mind was turning over everything he knew so far about the incidents of the past few days, but nothing was clear. He could not see a direct course of action which would bring him the results he desired. He went into the hotel and confronted the clerk, Bart Joiner, whom he knew well. Joiner was a small man, neatly dressed, his face smooth and rather pale.

'Bart, I know you keep your mouth shut about the people coming and going here, but I need to know a thing or two that might help me out in my work.'

Joiner glanced around the lobby, then leaned forward, speaking in an undertone.

'What's on your mind, Slade? Is it about Brady? He spent the night in Mrs Burden's room.'

'I knew that already,' Slade replied, grimacing. 'No, it's about Mrs Burden herself. She got off the train from Big Bend and booked in here. Can you tell me what she did after that?'

'Nothing far as I know, except entertain Brady all night. Why you interested in Lola, Slade?'

'Frank Burden figures I'm the man fooling around with Lola.'

'That could be fatal.'

'Yeah. I've come close to having a couple of run-ins with Burden over it. But I'm interested in Lola's movements. Did anyone else visit her room between the time she arrived and when Brady went up?'

'Not while I was on duty. But I had a couple of hours off during the early evening. Julie was standing in for me. If you hang on a couple of minutes I'll go ask her. She's in the kitchen.'

'Thanks, I'm obliged.'

The clerk returned, shaking his head, and Slade learned that only Phil Brady had gone along to Lola's room the evening before. He thanked the man and departed.

Brady was coming back along the street, and Slade studied the man as he waited for Brady to join him. He sighed heavily as he came to a sudden decision.

'Phil, I want you to go on to end of track as soon as you can,' he said. 'I'll explain the situation there. You take care of that trouble while I see what I can do about Rolph. Now listen carefully, and work with Chain Becker when you get there.'

He explained all that had taken place at end of track, and there was disappointment in Brady's face, but the man did not argue with Slade's decision. They parted then, and Slade went down to the depot to catch the first available train out of Las Corros.

It was dark when Slade reached Sourdough Creek, and he spent the rest of the night in the depot, arising at dawn to prepare for his ride. There was a horse waiting for him, and provisions already sacked. He was shown the scene of the robbery, and he checked it over carefully, paying particular attention to the tracks left by the robbers when they rode out. He went along to the small cemetery and stood bareheaded and silent by Harry Kelleher's grave for some moments, thinking about the man, recalling some of the things Harry had said, and his face was set in grim lines when he finally turned away, having made a vow that this death would be avenged, that the gang which brought it about would pay in full for what they had done.

CHAPTER EIGHT

When he rode out of Sourdough Creek on the track of half a dozen horses, Slade was tight-lipped and determined. He had made a study of the hoofprints around the right of way and glittering rails, and he would know most of the prints again no matter where he saw them. He had been well trained in the art of tracking by Hard Sam, and he rode steadily, his eyes watching the hard ground. He soon lost sight of the township and threaded his way through a narrow swale between two hills. He rode steadily through the morning, easily following the tracks, until he came to a spot where the tracks split up, three pairs of riders heading out in different directions. This was a favourite Drogo Rolph trick designed to lose pursuers. He studied the tracks intently, then turned off to check out the left hand pair.

After three miles he encountered rocky ground and the tracks ceased to exist. He wasted the better part of two hours before deciding to return to the spot where the tracks split. Reaching it, he set out on the trail of the pair of tracks moving to the right. Five miles later they, too, were lost in hard ground, and as he retraced his trail yet again, Slade knew he was not going to have any more luck this trip than he had found on any of the previous times he had trailed the Rolph gang.

The centre pair of tracks continued south-west, and after he had followed for several miles, Slade began to have hopes that they would not suddenly peter out, but he halted when they split, the two riders separating and moving in almost opposite directions.

He followed the left hand set of tracks first, and expected them to fade out of existence before very long, which they did on the first rocky outcrop. He crossed the rocks and cast around on the farther side of them, looking for the tracks to resume, but they did not, and he realized the outlaw had followed the rocks, and might have done so for miles before resuming his original direction.

Going back to where the split had occurred, he went through the ritual again, following the right hand tracks, and they led him a merry dance across the rough countryside. But they kept going, and he wondered why they had not been blotted out like all the others. He soon discovered why. He entered a valley through which a wide stream meandered, and the tracks entered the water and did not emerge on the other side. His quarry had gone up or downstream, and there was nothing to indicate to Slade which direction he should take.

He went upstream first, watching either side to see if the tracks suddenly began again, and he rode clear through the valley before deciding that his man had not come this way. Turning, he rode back and continued downstream, until he left the valley and encountered hard ground where the tracks finally disappeared.

It was almost evening, and Slade sat his mount and stared around, filled with exasperation. He considered himself to be a better-than-average tracker, but he had set out that morning trailing six men and finished up with nothing to show for his efforts, patience and hard work, except a bad temper and a mind filled with frustration.

When he finally gave up the intention of tracking Rolph's gang shadows were closing in, and he turned and headed for Jules Crossing. He rode into the town just before midnight, tired and hungry and out of humour. Putting his horse in the stable, he went along to the hotel and registered, dumping his gear and blowing the dust from his gun before leaving once more. He went along the street in the shadows, determined to get some good out of his day's work.

He found the Overland Freight Company's yard and corrals at the far end of the street, and there was a two storey house to one side, a light showing in one ground floor window. Going to the house, he knocked at the door, breathing heavily, trying to control his frustration over the failures of the day. The door was opened by a tall, thin man of middle age, whose lean face was set in a scowl.

'What the hell do you want at this time of the night?' the man greeted.

'I'm looking for a man called Harvey Trimble,' Slade said thinly. 'Know where I can find him? I figure he lives here because this place is next to the Freight Company's yard.'

'I'm Trimble, but I don't work day and night. If it's to do with business then come back in the morning, after eight.'

'It's to do with business okay,' Slade said through his teeth, further angered by the man's attitude, 'and it won't hold until tomorrow. I'm Slade Hollister, chief troubleshooter for Middle and Far Western Railroad. Maybe you've heard of us, huh? Well me and you have some talking to do, Trimble.'

The freighter made as if to slam the door in Slade's face, but Slade was ready for such a move and he slid a foot forward into the doorway. The door hit his toe and bounced back, smacking Trimble heavily in the face. The man cursed and fell back, lifting his hands to the door. He tried to slam it harder, and Slade leaned forward, taking it on his shoulder and sending it rebounding once more.

Slade reached for the butt of his gun. 'I'm ready to go all the way if you are, Trimble,' he rapped. 'But I got the impression that you prefer to get others to do your fighting. Now pull that gun and get it over with or drop the gunbelt on the floor and we'll talk instead. It's up to you which way it goes.'

Trimble looked into his expressionless face, then unbuckled his gunbelt, let it fall, and turned away from the door, towards his office. Slade entered the house, closed the door, and followed carefully, holstering his gun as he did so.

'What's this all about?' Trimble demanded when they were in the office. 'I'm not causing any trouble with the railroad. Hell, I'd be a fool to try. They're much too big for me to buck.'

'It's a different story I've heard from the hardcases you sent into our camp at end of track on the spur that's being pushed through here from Las Corros,' Slade said.

'Anyone told you I know something about it is lying,' Trimble said.

'Don't try that,' Slade retorted, grinning. 'You'd be surprised the number of men who do come it. All we have to do is take some of your hardcases to court and it's all over bar the shouting.'

'I got no hardcases working for me. I run a freight line. I don't have time to fool around with the kind of stuff you're talking about.'

'You telling me you never heard of a man called Cal Bland?' Slade demanded sharply. He paused, but knew by Trimble's face that he had got it right. 'Well Bland was in trouble at end of track. He knifed a man. He told me that you paid him to prevent the railroad completing the spur between here and Las Corros before you got some contracts signed. Now no man is gonna lie through his teeth about a thing like that, Trimble. You're back of the trouble we got, and if it doesn't stop right now then you're gonna find yourself in more trouble than you can get out of.'

There was bluster in Trimble's face, but he said nothing. Slade studied him for a moment, thinking over what he had said. He nodded slowly.

'I figure you can see the writing on the wall, Trimble. Now you better do something about those hardcases you hired. The last I heard Cal Bland talking, he was planning on blowing up all the trestles between end of track and Las Corros. Can you imagine the kind of trouble that destruction will cost you?'

'You better get out of here now,' Trimble said, but his voice had lost most of its truculence. 'I got a lot of work on my hands and you're interrupting it.'

'I'm on my way,' Slade told him. 'I just hope I don't have to come back to see you, Trimble.'

The man made no reply, and Slade departed, moving away from the house, then pausing in the shadows. Minutes later the door of the house was opened and Trimble appeared. He went fast along the street with Slade tailing him, and turned into the saloon. Slade moved in closer and peered through a window. The saloon was quiet, with barely a dozen men inside, and Trimble was talking to the bartender. Looking around at the rest of the men, most of whom were at the card tables, Slade received a shock, for one of them was Flash Dan Delmont.

As he watched, a footstep on the sidewalk nearby alerted Slade and he turned quickly, to find a man's figure looming up at his side.

'Don't move,' came a low warning. 'I got my gun on you. Who are you, mister, and why don't you find out what you want to know from inside the saloon?'

Slade grinned, for he recognized the tones, and he held his hands wide.

66

'Don't shoot, Marshal,' he said. 'I ain't breaking the law.'

'Slade Hollister? Is that you?' The town marshal came closer, peering into Slade's face. 'By thunder, it is you? What are you sneaking around my town for?'

'Howdy, Jake? I got some troubles I'm trying to whittle down, and most them stem from two of the men in the saloon.'

'Harv Trimble wouldn't be one of them, huh?' the marshal demanded.

'How would you know about that, Jake?'

'Hell, everyone in town is aware that Trimble will be put out of business soon as that spur line is finished. Trimble has been going around spouting about what he'll do to prevent the railroad finishing the line. What's he been up to?'

'I'll tell you shortly,' Slade replied. 'But right now I'm interested in what's going on in there. Take a look at Trimble.' He moved aside so the local lawman could peer through the window. 'See the man with him? Know who he is?'

'Yeah, I know him. He pulled in here yesterday with half a dozen hardcases and a dozen saloon girls. Tried to make a complaint to me about railroad men burning him out of his tents at end of track. Would you know anything about that, Slade?'

'I sure would. It was the easiest way of getting Delmont out of there. He's got some tough characters on his payroll.'

'You better be warned that he ain't done with you yet, Slade,' the lawman said. 'I've heard some of the threats flying around. You ain't the most popular man in this town.'

'That figures. Say, have you seen a hombre name of Cal Bland around here lately?'

'Sure. He's always in and out of town.'

'Who does he work for, apart from having signed on to work for the railroad!'

'Is that where he's been getting to lately?' The marshal sighed heavily. 'I might have guessed he was making a nuisance of himself somewhere. I've been thankful he ain't been around here for some weeks. But he used to work for Trimble.'

'I see.' Slade peered through the window, and saw Flash Dan Delmont getting to his feet. Delmont held out his hand and

Trimble, who arose instantly, grasped it and shook hands firmly.

He eased back from the window and moved to the alley beside the saloon when Trimble and Delmont came towards the batwings, and the marshal stood at his side until the two men had passed. He glanced in at the window again, and stiffened when he spotted one of the girls leaving a corner table and moving towards the bar.

'How long has she been here, Jake?' he demanded.

'That's Maisie. She's new here,' the town marshal replied. 'Not a bad looking gal. Do you know her?'

'Sure do!' Slade grinned tightly. 'The last time I saw her she was in one of Drogo Rolph's hideouts. You heard about Joe Wade getting killed, huh?'

'Yeah.'

'She was there when I killed him. He still had a sack of gold on his horse.'

'Well I'll be damned. Did you lose her?'

'No. I turned her loose, but wished I hadn't. She might be able to lead me to Drogo Rolph. I don't want to show my face in the saloon in case someone recognizes me, but you could go in there and bring her out, Jake. Tell her there's an old friend waiting to see her.'

'Sure. Anything to help the railroad, and I surely owe you a couple of big favours, Slade. Why don't you go over to my office and I'll bring Maisie there?'

'Good. I'll stay out of sight. I don't want anyone else getting a line on my whereabouts.'

The marshal chuckled and went into the saloon, and Slade went across the street to the law office. The street door was locked and he stood in the shadows, waiting patiently until he saw the big figure of the town marshal coming towards him, accompanied by Maisie Clapham. The girl was asking the marshal in high-pitched tones if she were being arrested or not.

'I told you, Maise, there's an old friend waiting to see you,' Jake McCall said easily.

Slade stepped out of the shadows when they arrived and confronted the girl, who peered at him in the uncertain light coming from the shaded law office window.

'Hi, Maisie,' Slade said. 'I didn't figure to run into you again so soon.'

'Who are you?' the girl demanded anxiously. 'I ain't done anything wrong. Am I being arrested?'

'I'm Slade Hollister. You must remember me, Maisie.'

'Oh sure. I'm never gonna forget you, Hollister. What do you want with me now?'

'I'm making a round of the town,' McCall said. 'You can talk in my office, Slade.' He unlocked the door and opened it. 'I won't be back for an hour.'

'Thanks. I'll do the same for you one day, Jake,' Slade replied. He motioned for Maisie to enter the office, then followed her and closed the door. For a moment he stood staring at her, seeing her once again as she had stood in the shack in the hide-out the day he killed Joe Wade. 'You're a real pretty gal, Maisie,' he mused aloud. 'What in hell are you doing working in a saloon? You could do better for yourself, I'm certain.'

'Oh yeah? I've heard that kind of talk before.' There was heavy sarcasm in the girl's tones, but she lifted a hand and patted her blonde hair, and there was a glint of appreciation in her pale blue eyes. 'But you haven't come all the way to Jules Crossing just to talk about me, Hollister. What is it you want?'

'I've come to see you, Maisie, because I figure you can do me favour. I did you one by turning you loose when I could have jailed you, and now I need your help.'

'If it's for what I think it is then the answer is no before you ask,' came the sharp reply. 'I don't know where Drogo is and I don't care. I didn't go to San Blanca when you let me go.'

'I know that,' he retorted. 'But my men were there and Drogo showed up. I lost a man. He was little more than a kid. Rolph killed him in a shootout.'

'Gee, I'm sorry.' There was genuine concern on the girl's painted face. 'But you know Drogo is like that. I was plenty scared of him most of the time I was around him. He can't lay off the drink, you know, and it does something to him inside. I seen him gun down his pet dog for the want of a target when he's had a new gun to try out. I don't want to get mixed up with him again, Hollister. He's loco, and ain't safe.'

'I don't want you to get mixed up with him, Maisie,' Slade

69

said patiently. 'Listen to what I've got to say. There's a big reward out on Rolph, and all you've got to do is tell me where he hides out at times. You don't have to take any risks, just give me information, and when Rolph is taken I'll see to it that you get a share of the reward.'

She laughed musically, shaking her head. 'It sounds like an interesting proposition, Hollister,' she said, 'and I'd go for it like a shot if you could guarantee that I'd live long enough to spend the dough. But Rolph has got a lot of friends, and some of them are in high places. He'd find out what had happened and one dark night I'd meet up with one of his friends and that would be the end of me.'

'Can you tell me anything at all that would give me something to work on?' he pleaded. 'Who are these friends of his? How does he get his information about which trains to rob and which to let go?'

'So you've found out that someone is passing him information, huh?' Maisie demanded.

'I worked it out,' he said grudgingly, 'but I don't have any idea who's doing it. Can you throw any light on it for me?'

Again she shook her head, and Slade took a deep breath then sighed heavily.

'Just think what you could do with maybe five thousand dollars, Maisie,' he prompted. 'You could have the time of your life.'

'It won't work, Hollister,' she said determinedly. 'I'm not sticking out my neck for you or anyone. If you figure to get Rolph then you'll have to be a whole heap smarter than you are right now.' She got to her feet. 'Now can I go?'

He nodded slowly. 'I guess I don't blame you,' he said. 'But watch yourself in future. It could be that Rolph might drop onto you around here. He's got his hideout someplace in the area, and if he does figure you've helped me he might do something about you.'

He opened the door for her, and for a moment he was silhouetted against the light that streamed out across the sidewalk. Then he stepped aside for Maisie to leave, and in that instant a series of gunflashes tattered the shadows across the street and a hail of bullets came splintering into the doorway. Slade felt the numbing shock of a hit in his left forearm as he hurled himself sideways at the girl, trying to push her out of harm's way. A stabbing lance of fire streaked across the back of his neck and another flashed alongside his right ribs. Dimly he heard the girl's high pitched scream of agony, and he rolled on the floor, dragging his gun clear of leather as he did so.

CHAPTER NINE

Slade was aware of pain burning through him as he got to his feet and reeled to a window. He smashed out the glass with the barrel of his big gun and stabbed the muzzle forward, cutting loose at the gun flashes across the street. He moved back to the door, his left arm useless at his side. Risking death, he lunged outside and moved to the right, flattening his straight back against the front wall of the building. He saw a shadowy figure running along the street and lifted his gun to cover it, yelling for the man to stop. The figure paused and swung around to face him, and a yellowish flash split the darkness. Slade heard the bullet strike woodwork by his right shoulder, and his lips peeled back from his teeth as he replied with a single aimed shot sent into the centre of his attacker's blossoming gunflash.

His eyes were dazzled by the flashes, but he moved instantly, going out to the street and hurrying towards the spot where his man had sagged into the dust. He blinked rapidly, barely able to see, but his target was out of the fight, stretched full length in the dust, sprawled lifelessly on his face. He kicked away the fallen gun that lay near to an outstretched hand, then turned slowly, studying his surroundings. A man was coming at a run towards him along the street, and already there were shadowy figures moving on the sidewalks.

'Declare yourself.' Slade's harsh voice cut through the dying echoes of the shooting.

'Marshall McCall,' came the instant reply. 'Is that you, Slade?'

Slade heaved a long sigh, holstering his gun. He gripped his left forearm as the town marshal came up, and spoke through clenched teeth when asked for a report.

The marshal bent over the lifeless figure in the dust and struck a match. Slade peered down, but could not get a good look at the features. McCall uttered a curse, then straightened, his face just a blur in the darkness.

'That's Cal Bland,' he said sharply. 'Trimble didn't take long to set his dogs on you.'

'There's another one opposite the jail,' Slade said. 'You go check him out, Jake. Maisie took a slug in the shooting. I heard her cry out.'

McCall cursed and went on across the street to a point opposite the jail, and Slade hurried into the law office, pausing on the threshold to stare down at the body of Maisie Clapham. There was blood on the front of the girl's dress. He dropped to one knee and examined her, heaving a sigh of relief when he found that she was still breathing. He straightened and turned to the door as McCall appeared, carrying a wounded man.

'You didn't waste any time taking care of these two,' Jake McCall said. 'This one is still breathing, but Cal Bland is dead. I want Trimble now.' He eased his burden to the floor and peered at the unconscious girl. 'How is Maisie?'

'She's still breathing, but she'll need a doctor pronto. I'll go pick up Trimble for you,' he said, looking into the marshal's grim face. 'I figure he's got some talking to do, especially after we saw him talking to Flash Dan Delmont. I reckon he's mixed up in this somewhere.'

'I'd be obliged if you would start cleaning up while I take care of this,' McCall said. 'Bring Trimble in dead or alive. He's been threatening to cause trouble for some time now, and he's got to be stopped.'

Slade drew his gun, checking it carefully. He reholstered the weapon and strode out to the street, moving away quickly through the crowd of men beginning to gather outside the law office. He went along to Trimble's house, steeling himself when he saw a light in a ground floor window.

He did not knock at the door but entered swiftly, moving to Trimble's office, making no sound as he did so. He kicked open the office door and confronted Trimble and Flash Dan Delmot sitting at the table inside, both drinking whisky. They started to their feet at sight of Slade, Trimble's face turning pale. Delmont merely tightened his lips, but his smooth manner slowly deserted him, his eyes showing something of the apprehension gripping him.

'Okay, Trimble,' Slade rapped, his hand on the butt of his

holstered gun. 'And you, Delmont. The town marshal wants to talk to the both of you.'

'You've no authority here,' Delmont protested. 'This is not railroad right of way.'

Slade drew his gun so fast that both men blinked in surprise.

'This is the only authority I need,' he said through his teeth. 'Let's get going, shall we?'

'What the hell for?' Trimble cursed. 'If McCall wants to see me he knows where I live.'

'He told me to take you in dead or alive,' Slade rasped. 'I don't care which way it is.'

Trimble tightened his lips and moved to the door. Slade barred his way. The freighter paused and stared at him fear beginning to show in his lean features.

'Get rid of your gun, just so you won't be tempted to try and pull it,' Slade said. He waited until Trimble had complied, then looked at Delmont. 'I assume you are wearing a shoulder holster,' he rapped. 'If you are then empty it, Delmont, or I'll drop you in your tracks.'

Delmont carefully opened his coat and lifted a short-barrelled .38 out of a shoulder holster. He tossed it at Slade, who let it fall to the floor.

'Now let's be on our way,' Slade said. 'You both know where the jail is.'

The two men preceded him, and as they reached the front door, with Slade at their heels, a man appeared, his face taut, his eyes wide with excitement.

'Bland didn't pull it off, boss!' the newcomer exclaimed. 'He's lying dead in the street, and Hollister ain't dead.'

'Jake McCall will be pleased to hear you repeat that,' Slade said, showing himself from behind Delmont. 'Get rid of your gun, hombre, and join your boss on a walk to jail.'

The man was startled, but unable to do much about the situation with Slade's ready gun covering him. He unbuckled his gunbelt and walked ahead with Trimble and Delmont, and they went to the jail. The doctor was inside, working on Maisie, who was still unconscious. McCall picked up his keys and went to the rear of the office, where a large cell was situated. He locked the three prisoners inside, warning them to remain silent

74

when Trimble and Delmont began to protest. Delmont demanded to see a lawyer.

Slade went to look at the unconscious man who had been shooting at him from across the street, and he recognized the face. He was grim as he looked at Jake McCall

'Jake, this is one of the men Chain Becker fired from his gang at end of track the day Cal Bland knifed him. This one and several others were with Bland, planning to blow up the track and some of the trestle bridges, all on Trimble's sayso. I heard them talking it over myself, so you can have my evidence any time you need it.'

'I've done nothing against the railroad, and if anyone said I did then he's lying for some reason or other,' Trimble called from the cell.

'You've got nothing against me,' Flash Dan snapped. 'Even if Trimble is mixed up in anything local, I ain't got nothing to do with it. I was talking to him in the saloon, making a deal for the wagons and gear I salvaged from the fire out at end of track that destroyed everything I owned. I ain't broke no law that I know of.'

The doctor got to his feet from Maisie's side and came to confront Slade and the marshal. His lined face was grave, and Slade tightened his lips.

'What about her, Doc?'

'She's got a fair chance if she's carefully nursed.'

'If she dies then there'll be a murder charge against Trimble,' Slade said, and McCall nodded eagerly.

'You better strip off your shirt and sit down,' the doctor told Slade. 'Let me take care of you. You're bleeding in several places.'

Slade was helped out of his shirt, and he sat down wearily, clenching his teeth at the doctor's ministrations. But his wounds were dressed, and McCall gave him a clean shirt when he had been bandaged.

'Your left arm is the most serious wound,' the doctor said. 'Try and rest it up, Hollister.'

'Yeah, I'll leave it behind in town when I ride out for end of track,' Slade retorted. 'Thanks, Doc. I guess the railroad will pay your bill.'

'You ain't riding out tonight, Slade,' said McCall. 'You'd

never make it. Why don't you bed down in my cot in the backroom? Come morning you'll feel more like riding out, and there might be something breaking around here that you'll need to know about.'

Slade nodded slowly.

'I reckon I'll take you up on that offer,' he said tiredly. 'I figure I'd fall off my horse if I rode out now. But do me one last favour, Jake. Send a wire to Big Bend explaining all this to Hard Sam and tell him I'm making for end of track tomorrow from Jules Crossing. Ask him to contact me here before seven in the morning if there is anything come up that I should know about.'

'Leave it to me,' McCall said. 'Now you get yourself some sleep. I'll handle everything around here.'

Slade went through to the small backroom and flopped down upon the bed, closing his eyes and relaxing thankfully. Despite the nagging pain of his wounds he sank into slumber almost immediately, and knew no more until Jake McCall roused him up next morning and thrust a cup of coffee into his hands.

'I hope you're feeling better than you look, Slade,' the marshal said with a grin that was taut and mirthless. 'I had to turn Delmont loose in the night. There was nothing against him, and I let him see the local lawyer, who got him out with no trouble at all. But I'm holding Trimble and he's in bad trouble. That hombre you hit last night when you killed Cal Bland is in a bad way, and he talked some about what was going on. He said his name is Scully. He was fired from the railroad by Becker when you showed up there. He reckons Bland recruited him and some of the others to cause all the trouble the railroad is getting on the spur line. He says Trimble was paying for it.'

'Is he likely to live to give evidence?'

'The Doc reckons he will.'

'What about Maisie?' There was a sharp note in Slade's voice.

'She's got a good chance if there's no infection,' McCall said. 'I hope she'll pull through, Slade.'

'So do I. Keep an eye on her for me, Jake, and I'll be in your debt.'

'You'll never be in my debt, not after what you did here last night, as if I didn't already owe you a lot, Slade. But Hard Sam replied to the wire I sent him last night. He said there's no news of the Rolph gang. The gold shipment has disappeared without trace. Frank Burden is calling for your suspension because you haven't handled the job right since you took over from Sam.'

Slade smiled grimly. 'I'll sort that out when I get back to Big Bend,' he said. 'Did you tell Sam I was going to end of track today?'

'Yeah. He'll contact you there if anything else comes up.'

'You can reach me by sending a wire to Big Bend,' Slade said. 'But I'll be in touch with you, Jake. When I'm at end of track I'll see if I can round up the rest of the gang Cal Bland gathered about him. Keep me informed about Maisie, huh?'

'You can rely on it,' McCall told him. 'Watch your step though, Slade. Flash Dan Delmont makes a bad enemy, and he wasn't happy about the way you handled him last night. He swears it was you burned him out at end of track.'

'Well he's right about that,' Slade replied grimly, 'and if he starts anything around me I'll burn him with a slug or two.'

He rode out and headed for end of track, and the morning passed as his mount carried him tirelessly across the ground that would shortly carry the rails intended to link Jules Crossing with Las Corros. The surveyors had already been over the route and their markers showed clearly. Slade followed them, impatient as the miles dropped behind him, and the sun burned down ceaselessly, making his thoughts hard to control. But he mused over what had happened and what was likely to happen, trying to find one man who could reasonably be suspected of working for the robbers. He kept discarding Frank Burden's name, and Phil Brady's, but his suspicions of them remained and he could not satisfy himself either way about their position in the whole situation.

A rifle cracked and dust spurted a foot in front of his mount. Slade looked up quickly, his sixgun leaping into his hand as he stared around for trouble, and the flat echoes of the shot chased away to the horizon, the sounds telling him that a rifle was at work. He swung out of his saddle and hunted cover, and as he dropped flat in a depression in the hard, sunbaked ground, a second bullet tugged at the brim of his hat. His horse galloped away some fifty yards before halting, and Slade stared after the animal, his lips pulled taut in a wry smile. His Winchester was still in the saddleboot!

He lay still as shot after shot was blasted at his position. But he was covered and the shooting did not worry him.

When at last it dropped away to desultory shots, then faded altogether, Slade removed his hat and peered out from his cover. He saw a horseman on a rise some two hundred yards out, and another man, on foot and holding a rifle, was standing beside the rider. They were talking animatedly. Slade tightened his grip upon his sixgun and waited. There was nothing he could do until they drew within range of his handgun.

Presently the second man fetched his horse, and the two riders came into the open and advanced towards the spot where Slade was lying, evidently under the impression that he had been hit and was out of action. He lay watching them, his teeth pulled back from his lips in a snarl, and when they did not separate for safety he cocked his gun and tensed for action. When the men drew nearer he recognized them as two of the workers who had been fired by Chain Becker.

Then one of the men swung away to collect Slade's horse, and the other kept coming. He was twenty yards out when Slade pushed himself up to one knee and levelled his Colt. The rider yelled and threw up his gun, and Slade shot him in the chest, getting to his feet and running forward as the man tumbled out of his saddle.

The other rider was almost at the spot where Slade's horse was standing, and he wheeled around at the shot, lifting his rifle quickly. Slade reached the horse, stepping over the fallen rider, and he snatched the man's rifle from its saddleboot. A rifle cracked and the bullet struck the horse. Slade was knocked flying as the animal fell, and he rolled over and over, clutching the rifle desperately. There was another shot at him before he came to rest, but he was not touched, and when he pushed himself into a sitting position he saw the other rider swinging away and making a run for it.

Slade took swift aim, swinging the rifle to allow for movement. He fired at the man, saw him jerk under the impact, and reloaded quickly. When the rider did not come down out of his saddle he fired again, and this time the man threw wide his arms and plunged sideways. The horse ran on for a hundred yards before stopping.

Pushing himself wearily to his feet, Slade limped back to where the nearer man lay, and found he was dead, shot through the heart. Checking the fallen horse, Slade found the beast hard hit and dying. He drew his Colt and sent a bullet through the animal's brain. Then he walked slowly across to where his own mount was standing with trailing reins. Nearby the second man lay dead.

Slade mounted and rode on. He had no time to collect the bodies. He figured both men had been on their way to Jules Crossing to check with Cal Bland or Trimble, and they had spotted him and tried for him, a mistake which cost them their lives.

Slade rode through the late afternoon, making for the end of track, riding easily over the ground that had been prepared for the gleaming rails pushing out from Las Corros. The shadows were long upon the ground when he finally came in sight of the construction camp, and he reined up, taking a deep breath as he stared at the familiar scene.

Riding closer, he saw Chain Becker directing the laying of the last rails of the day. The sun was low upon the horizon, the brassy sky tinted crimson and gold. Becker was standing by the newly laid ties, and under his skilled direction twelve men were carrying a section of rail from the flat car at the end of the completed track and lowering it into position on the ties. Other men were following closely, driving in spikes, tamping down earth and bolting rails together. There was one last rail section on the flat car and it was unloaded and carried forward. Becker's voice was harsh and commanding in the surrounding silence.

'Up! Forward! Ready! Down!'

Becker had spotted Slade's arrival, and now the big man came across to stand at Slade's stirrup, peering up in the growing gloom at Slade's taut features.

'Glad to see you, Slade,' the camp boss greeted.

'Hi, Chain. Had any trouble around here?'

'Someone took some shots at the camp just after dawn,' came

the grim reply. 'But Phil Brady showed up and went out on a search. There's been no trouble since.'

'I got a couple of your men, I reckon,' Slade said, and dismounted slowly, favouring his left arm. He explained to Becker what had happened, both on the trail and in Jules Crossing the previous night.

'I got some more trouble here,' Becker went on. 'It's over in the passenger car behind my coach. I put her in the passenger car behind my coach, seeing she's the Area Manager's wife. I don't know why the hell she came up from Las Corros on the work train, Slade, but she's here and smouldering like a damp fire.'

'Lola Burden.' Slade frowned as he stared into Becker's face.

'The same. I don't feel easy when she's around, Slade. The way she looks at a man, I figure she's eating him, like a tigress, or a she-mountain cat.'

'Yeah, well as long as she stays clear of me then I don't care where she goes,' Slade said. 'I'll put my horse away, Chain, and I'd better wait around until Brady shows up again. I want him.'

'He wasn't in the best frame of mind when he showed up,' Becker commented. 'His face was all bruised up. Looked like he lost an argument with a mule's hind leg.'

Slade grinned tightly as he rode on into camp, and he dismounted outside the rope corral and took care of his mount. As he turned the animal into the corral he caught a glimpse of a horse he recognized, standing still saddled near the passenger car on the loop-line behind Becker's coach. It was Brady's horse. Slade tightened his lips, for Lola Burden was in that coach, and it looked as if Brady had known about her arrival. He started forward into the shadows, for the soft darkness of night was stealing in gently around the sprawling camp, and as he neared the coach a window in it was suddenly thrust wide and a figure came leaping clear, falling heavily upon the ground before springing up and leaping into the saddle of the waiting horse.

The rider galloped away, and Slade bent at the knees to get a silhouette for a moment, recognized Brady instantly. His face was hard as he went onto the coach, and as he grasped the brass rail on the observation platform at the rear and began to mount the steps, the door of the coach opened and a man appeared on the platform. Lanternlight streamed out and shone full upon Slade's face. The man let out an enraged yell, and Slade recognized the voice immediately. It was Frank Burden himself. Before he could say or do anything, Burden lashed out with a heavy boot, taking Slade in the face, and Slade went over backwards and fell insensible to the ground.

CHAPTER TEN

Water splashing into Slade's face brought him back to his senses, and he groaned as he pushed himself into a sitting position. There was pain in his face and his lips seemed swollen to twice their normal size. His head throbbed dully, and for a moment he stared around dazedly, trying to recollect his scattered wits. Lola Burden was standing near him, in the light issuing from the coach, and there was a pail of water in her hands, the contents of which she was flicking over Slade with a cupped hand. In the background two men were wrestling, one shouting and cursing vilely.

Slade recalled what had happened and pushed himself upright, used his left arm without thinking, and sprawled sideways on his face as the wounded limb refused to take his weight. He was filled with anger when he finally got to his feet and started towards the two men, and he recognized the shouting voice as Frank Burden's. The second man, he quickly saw, was Chain Becker, and the big camp boss, because of the knife wound he had taken from Cal Bland, was having great difficulty preventing Burden using a gun on Slade. He was losing his hold on Burden's gunhand.

'I'll kill you, Hollister,' Burden yelled stridently. 'I've figured all along it was you seeing Lola, and now I caught you. I got you dead to rights. I told Lola I was arriving here at end of track tomorrow and she came on to wait for me, but I knew I'd get here tonight. I tricked her and caught you.'

Slade reached the two men, aware that half the workers in the camp had been attracted by Burden's frenzied yelling. He reached out with his right hand and wrenched the gun out of Burden's hand, handing it to Becker as the camp boss stepped away from the Area Manager.

'You've gone too far this time, Frank,' Slade said in a cold fury. 'I warned you back in Big Bend not to come for me again with Lola as the problem.'

82

Slade swing his right first and connected with Burden's jaw, the force of the blow jarring through his wrist to the elbow. But he might have waved a feather duster under the Area Manager's nose for all the good the blow seemed to do. Burden bellowed wildly and started punching, bullying his way forward, crashing his solid fists into Slade's body.

The bullet wounds he had taken the night before were still painful, and their effect upon Slade's physical condition was apparent when he tried to fight. His left arm was useless, and when he lifted it to block some of Burden's wilder swings the Area Manager's big right fist connected with it, numbing it from wrist to elbow. If he'd had the use of both hands and all his strength he would easily have beaten the older man, but he could not punch with his left hand and he found himself getting the worst of the terrific exchanges. His ribs on the right felt sticky, where a bullet had gouged flesh from the bones, and he knew the wound had reopened. He was filled with desperation, but he remained cool, and as Burden came roaring in once more Slade lowered his head, ducked beneath the big man's guard, and butted him in the stomach.

At fifty years of age, Frank Burden was already beginning to feel the pace. In his prime he had been the chief troubleshooter for the railroad, but the years had climbed steadily upon Burden's shoulders. His legs were rubbery, his breathing faulty. The unexpected head butt into his midriff robbed the older man of his power. He staggered, and Slade straightened again and slugged away with his right hand, throwing a flurry of punches against Burden's jaw.

Slade was almost out on his feet. There was a singing in his ears and his sight was suddenly unreliable. He found it difficult to judge the distance between them, and several of his blows were short. But he had almost twenty years on his side, and when he sensed Burden was faltering he renewed his attempts to knock the man down. He struck solidly, shrewdly, and suddenly Burden was no longer standing before him and Chain Becker was pushing forward, taking hold of Slade and supporting him.

There was a buzzing in Slade's ears, and coloured lights seemed to flash crazily before his eyes. His legs were trembling, rubbery, threatening to let him down, and there was pain in every part of his body. His face felt as if it had been run down by a train.

'Somebody pick up Burden and put him in that coach,' Becker yelled stridently. 'And make him stay there. Take a gun to him if you have to. That's an order. I'll be back in a spell to see to him.'

'I'm okay,' Slade said, thrusting Becker away. 'I want to talk to Burden myself.'

'Who was it came out that window?' Becker demanded. 'I saw him and the horse. I saw you going towards the coach. Who was it, Slade?'

'Forget it,' Slade retorted, shaking his head. His teeth ached and there were darting pains in his head. His mouth was swollen, his lips stiff, making his words sound stilted. He swayed as he turned to Burden, and two men were trying to revive the Area Manager.

Slade went to where Lola was standing, still clutching the bucket, and he snatched it from her, crossing to Burden and tossing its contents into the man's face. Burden came back to his senses, cursing and spluttering, and in the gloom that surrounded them he stared up at Slade.

'Get on your feet,' Slade snapped, and Burden had to make several attempts to do so. When he was erect he leaned back against the coach, drawing great gulps of air into his palpitating lungs. The sound of his laboured breathing was harsh in the silence. 'I want to talk to you,' Slade went on. 'Get in the coach. That's an order. Get in there and keep your mouth shut. You too, Lola.'

The woman came forward without hesitation and ascended the steps, disappearing into the car. Burden looked as if he would not obey, but Slade took hold of his elbow and forced the man around. Burden pulled back for a moment, but his strength was gone and he was feeling his age. He climbed with difficulty and went into the coach. Slade followed, turning to motion for Becker to join them.

Inside the coach Lola sat down in a corner, her eyes downcast. Burden went to a table where there were bottles of whisky, and he poured himself a stiff drink. He staggered to a seat and dropped into it, almost falling to the floor, and Slade stood with his back to a wall, his body trembling, his mind weary, his senses battered along with the rest of him. Chain Becker entered the coach and slammed the door. The camp boss was also angry by what had occurred, and his face proclaimed the fact.

'Let's get this straight,' Slade said stiffly, and Burden looked up at him, hatred in his face. 'I was not the man who left this coach by the window.' He went onto explain what had happened without mentioning that he had recognized Phil Brady. 'I was coming to see what was going on when you came out of the coach, Burden, and you put two and two together and came up with the wrong answer.'

'I came into the coach from the other end,' Burden said thickly. There was blood trickling from a corner of his mouth and his lips were slack. His face was pale, as if the shock and strain of the incident and the fight had been too much for him. 'I saw a man leaving by the window. When I saw you coming up those steps I figured I'd got you to rights. But if it wasn't you then who in hell was it?'

'I figure Lola can tell you that,' Becker snapped from the doorway. 'I know it wasn't Slade because I spoke to him when he rode into camp, and he was putting his horse in the corral when that hombre lit out of the coach window. Frank, you're way out on a limb, and you owe Slade a big apology. Hell, you fought him and he was shot up last night in Jules Crossing. He was hit by three slugs.'

'What happened in Jules Crossing?' Burden demanded. 'I got a lot to talk to you about Rolph's getaway with that bullion from the San Blanca eight-fifteen. That's quite apart from the fact that Harry Kelleher was killed.'

Slade moved to the table and poured himself a stiff drink, then sat down wearily opposite the Area Manager. Becker remained by the doorway, still angry. Slade explained his activities from the moment he rode out of Sourdough Creek on the trail of Rolph, and when he described losing the trail Burden began to shake his head and curse softly. When Slade lapsed into silence Burden took a deep breath.

'You did good in Jules Crossing,' he said grudgingly. 'But why in hell didn't Brady make that San Blanca train at Apache Well like he said he would?'

Slade explained that too, and watched Lola's hard face for

expression as he did so, but the woman was not listening to their conversation. Burden listened intently, and then pushed himself to his feet and came to the table to refill his glass.

'There are several aspects of this business that I'm not satisfied with, Hollister,' he said a trifle pompously. 'For one thing, I've received a complaint and a demand for compensation from one Daniel Delmont for the destruction of his tented saloons adjacent to railroad land. Delmont claims he has witnesses who can swear that you fired his tents.'

'Just a minute, Frank,' Chain Becker cut in angrily. 'There ain't a man could have handled the situation here better than Slade did, not even Hard Sam himself. And as for the fire, well Slade and me were together when that happened, so any witnesses Delmont comes up with are lying.'

'That's only a part of it,' Burden went on ponderously. 'I don't figure you're doing enough about Drogo Rolph and his gang, Hollister. He should be your main objective. Since you've taken over your father's job you've lost two good men and let Rolph get away with a hundred thousand dollars in gold.'

Slade clenched his teeth on the angry retort that rose to his lips.

'There's another thing,' Burden went on inexorably. 'I've come to the conclusion that someone in the know is passing on the vital information about our gold shipments to Rolph.' He stared at Slade to discover his reaction, and Slade remained expressionless. 'That doesn't seem to surprise you any,' he snapped.

'I wouldn't know anything about that,' Slade said not wishing to divulge what he knew about that particular subject. 'I'm going out to get Rolph and his gang, and it won't matter a damn who's been feeding him information.'

'You reckon you're suddenly going to get lucky?' Burden sneered. 'I'll tell you this much, Hollister. Whether you're Hard Sam's son or not. If you don't soon come up with something good concerning Rolph then you're gonna find yourself out of a job.'

'And you'd take great pleasure in getting me fired,' Slade agreed. 'I figure we've gone through the business as far as it goes, so now you listen to me, Frank, and get it good. I warned you in Big Bend what would happen if you came for me just one more time over your wife. Okay, so I'm big-hearted, and I feel like stretching a point or two. I feel sorry for you, tied to Lola. But don't make this mistake again. You come for me once more and you better be carrying a gun. I don't take from any man what you did to me tonight.'

'If I have cause to come for you again it will be with a gun,' Burden rasped, getting angry. 'You better get out of here now. I don't even want to look at you.'

'That cuts both ways.' Slade turned to the door and Becker stepped aside for him. 'Frank, you and me better keep well clear of one another in future.'

Becker followed Slade out into the darkness, and the camp boss paused when they were out of earshot of the coach.

'If Burden has his way you'll be through around the railroad quicker than you know, Slade, even though Burden is coming down hard on Lola now. I didn't know he'd arrived here. He must have stopped his train outside of camp and walked in.'

'Looks like his private coach is coming in now,' Slade said, peering down the track. There was the sound of an engine coming towards them. 'I'd better eat and get cleaned up. I've got some more business to attend to.' He was thinking of Phil Brady as he spoke.

'Come and eat with me,' Becker invited. 'I don't suppose you'll get an invite from Burden.'

Slade smiled grimly as he walked with the camp boss to the cook shack, where men were already bellying up for hot food. But he paused when he spotted the white cover of an old prairie schooner standing to one side of the track.

'Chain, is that old Banjo's wagon?' he demanded.

'Sure is. He pulled in this afternoon, loaded with gear. I figure he's about sold out by now, and if he's sober come morning he'll pull out again.'

'I'll see you later. I got to have a talk with Banjo,' Slade said.

'I'll keep some grub by for you,' Becker promised, continuing on his way.

Slade went across to the wagon, where a small campfire burned on the sheltered side of it. He saw two figures seated at the fire, and one of them got up immediately his shadow moved through the darkness.

'Who's there?' a gruff old voice demanded, and Slade smiled as he stared hard at the old man seated by the fire.

'Slade Hollister,' he replied. 'I ain't seen you around in a coon's age, Banjo. Where you been hiding yourself?'

'Talk to Charlie, not me,' the oldster replied harshly. 'I got nothing to say to you, Hollister.'

'Take it easy, Grandpa,' the other said, coming forward to confront Slade. 'This is Slade, not Hard Sam.'

'Huh! I don't figure there's much difference between father and son,' the old man retorted, sniffing. 'They both eat, sleep, drink and breathe railroad.'

'How are you, Charlie?' Slade said, moving around until he could get the flickering firelight shining on the face of the tall, slender girl who stood before him. She was dressed in levis and a plaid shirt, with a flat crowned plains hat stuck atop her dark curly hair.

'Call me Charlene and I'll talk to you, Slade Hollister,' she replied, but her teeth glinted in a smile, and Slade felt his bad humour dissolving as he nodded slowly.

'Okay, that's a deal,' he said. 'Where you been hiding this old desert rat, Charlene?'

'We've been north for a spell,' she said. 'But I heard you took over your Pa's job. Had several run-ins with Drogo Rolph too, huh?'

'Some,' he admitted.

'That dratted polecat should have been hanged a long time ago,' old Banjo said with a string of mild curses to emphasize his words. 'We ran into him last week and he done smashed my banjo on account I didn't have no whisky for him.'

'Where did you see Rolph?' Slade demanded, immediately alert.

'We are about to sit and eat supper,' the old man retorted. 'You're welcome to join us if you promise not to talk business, Slade. You should know better than to ask me about the folks we meet on our travels. If I opened my mouth once I'd wake up one morning and find my throat cut.'

'I ain't eaten yet,' Slade said slowly. 'I'd be obliged if you would feed me, and I could surely do with having a serious talk with you, Banjo.'

'Come and sit down by the fire,' the girl said, her eyes shining as she took hold of Slade's arm. 'It's been too long since I saw you, Slade. I had to jaw Grandpa's ear off to get him to come back this way.'

'Hard Sam ran me out,' the old man reminded her. 'I'm taking a chance coming back here like this, but it's only on account of us hearing that Hard Sam is leaving the area. You ain't so bad, son,' he added, grinning toothlessly at Slade.

'What's brought you back?' Slade demanded.

'Business, amongst things,' Charlene said, turning to the fire, where a big pot was suspended above the flickering flames. A blackened coffee pot was bubbling merrily, and Slade sat down thankfully. 'I wanted to see you, Slade, and Grandpa figured we had to come because he reckons he ain't got much longer to live.'

'So where do I come in?' Slade asked.

'Hell, you always been sweet on Charlie,' old Banjo retorted. 'I figure to make it worth your while to wed the gal. I got to see she's well taken care of before I lay down and die. She's kind of sweet on you too, Slade, and mebbe the two of you can make a go of it. I brung her to you, son, like I told you a long time ago that I would. Now what do you say, before you eat my food at my fire? Will you take her off my hands?'

Slade looked at the girl, ready to laugh, for he imagined this was a joke. But Charlene Riley was watching him intently, her face expressing great seriousness, and he frowned as he recalled that there had always been a standing joke between them in the past, that when old Banjo Riley got too old to continue his living by travelling the country with his wagon full of dry goods for sale then Slade would marry Charlene and take her off the oldster's hands.

'Well?' the girl demanded, her pretty face taut with concern. 'You ain't going back on your word, Slade Hollister, are you?'

'Well,' he retorted. 'I'll tell you what I will consider. You give me some idea where Drogo Rolph hangs out these days and I might just take that old joke of ours serious.'

'You hear that, Grandpa?' the girl demanded instantly. 'Now's your chance. Tell Slade we saw them outlaws toting that gold they stole and he will wed me.'

Slade caught his breath at the words, for he could not believe he was hearing them right. But the whiskered old man leaned forward, his face ruddy in the firelight, and he stared at Slade for some moments while he reflected upon the deal. Then he nodded abruptly, chuckling harshly.

'It's a deal,' he said. 'I'll risk my life to get Charlie a good home. But you got to promise to make no mistakes in wiping out them outlaws, for if they ever lay their hands on me if you fail then I'll die slow and painful.'

'It's a promise,' Slade said without hesitation. He would have promised them the moon to get the information he needed. 'The day I put an end to Drogo Rolph and his gang I'll come right up to Charlie and ask her to marry me.'

CHAPTER ELEVEN

'Let's get down to business,' Slade said briskly. 'Banjo, if you saw Drogo's gang toting gold bullion then I want to know about it, and pronto. Where was this?'

'I got your word about Charlie?' the oldster demanded insistently.

'Banjo, I'd marry you if you can give me any information about those outlaws,' Slade retorted.

The girl laughed musically, and Slade looked at her searchingly in the light of the fire. She was around twenty-eight, he knew, and she was a pretty girl, tall and dark and slender, and the only time he had seen her in a dress at a dance somewhere she had really looked something. But he had never considered her as anything but a friend, and now he knew he might have to marry her.

'Well it was like this,' Banjo said, running long, gnarled fingers through his straggly whiskers. 'We come upon Rolph and half a dozen men in the hills north of Sourdough Creek. They was camped in the old Ross horse ranch. At first I figured we was in bad trouble, for Rolph has got some new men in his outfit and they figured to have some fun at Charlie's expense. But I been mighty useful to Drogo Rolph over the years, although mebbe I shouldn't tell you that, seeing as how you and your old man have been nigh busting your guts trying to catch Drogo.'

'Never mind that,' Slade said impatiently. 'Get on with it, Banjo. If you know where Rolph is holed up then tell me so I can get after him.'

'Well Rolph was resting up at the old Ross place, but that ain't where he's hiding out. I very likely could name a score of places where he might be and still not pick the right one. But if you go to the Ross place you'll be able to find tracks going on from there. No one can blot out tracks like Rolph, and he always beats you by doing just that after a raid. But when he's clear of the robbery area he don't bother too much with tracks, and you could nail him if you could get on his trail from the Ross place.'

'How many men you say Rolph has got with him?' Slade demanded. He was impatient to be moving out, but he wanted all the information he could get.

'Maybe half a dozen. Like I told you, he's got some new hands, but I saw Mulie Johnson with him, Bull Seymour and Abe Wensum. They said you killed Ned Bunch the other day.'

'Uhuh.' Slade nodded, his face grim in the firelight. He watched Charlene at the cooking pot, and when the girl handed him a plate of stew he tasted it and then praised her cooking.

'You just wait until I get in a real house and have a proper stove to work over,' she promised him. 'I'll keep your stomach happy when we're hitched, Slade.'

He made no comment, and after they had eaten he took his leave, going back to the camp to look for Brady. He found Becker in his office, and Phil Brady was there, sitting on a corner of the camp boss's desk. There were ugly bruises on Brady's face, and he was a little sheepish when he met Slade's gaze.

'I heard you had no luck after Rolph,' Brady said. His dark eyes were bright and watchful.

'I had no luck anywhere,' Slade answered. 'I even took a beating for you, Phil.' He explained how he had seen Brady leaping out the coach window and riding off. 'This is the last time I tell you to keep in line. After this you're in trouble.' He cut short the man's protests and continued sharply. 'Tomorrow we're riding out after Drogo Rolph. Be ready to ride soon as the sun shows.'

'Are you onto something?' Becker demanded.

'I don't want to talk about it, Chain,' Slade said tightly. 'There's been too many leaks in our outfit so far. We are riding out tomorrow and with any luck we should be able to come up with Rolph and half a dozen of his men in a couple of days. I don't want to send word of this to Big Bend yet, so maybe you'll give me two days before wiring Hard Sam about it, Chain? Like I said, I don't want any leakage of information this time.'

'Leave it to me,' the camp boss assured him. 'And if Sam wants to contact you?'

'Tell him I'm on an urgent job and he'll have to wait until I can get in touch with him.'

'I'll go get some sleep then,' Brady said, moving towards the door. 'Shall I pack supplies for a few days?' He eyed Slade intently.

'Yeah. About a week. There's no telling how long we'll be.' Slade sighed heavily as Brady departed, and when the man had gone Chain Becker shook his head.

'There's something about that hombre I don't cotton to, Slade,' he said. 'Do you have any trouble with him apart from his business of Lola Burden?'

'No. He's always done his duty properly. I've noticed there is something in the background with Brady, but I've never been able to put a finger on it. I'm watching him very carefully now, and if he puts a foot wrong he'll be out on his neck.'

'You've got to watch out for Burden,' Becker warned. 'He's in a killing mood, Slade.'

'I'll watch him.' Slade moved to the door. 'I'd better get some sleep too. I feel like I been dragged ten miles by a runaway horse. I've got a lot to do in the next few days, but with any luck Drogo Rolph should be finished.'

'Good luck,' Becker told him. 'I hope it goes the way you plan.'

Slade left the car and paused in the darkness to look around. He saw a figure moving along the side of the car, and bent a little to get it outlined. A woman! He became alert immediately. Was it Lola? His first impulse was to go and check, but he had no wish of being caught in her company by Frank Burden, and as he stood watching her, another figure appeared and joined her. It wasn't Burden, he realized, for it was the wrong shape, and he clenched his teeth as he figured it was Brady. He started after the couple, intent upon stamping out the trouble that would surely come if Phil Brady persisted in his association with another man's wife.

But when he caught up with them, easing forward in the darkness, he realized it was not Lola Burden, and the man was not Phil Brady. The woman's voice sounded in a musical laugh, and Slade recognized it as Charlene Riley's. Slade moved in closer to where the couple had halted in the shadows and he heard the man's voice, deep and impatient, echoing slightly in the darkness.

'Did Slade Hollister go for it?'

'I was just listening to him talking to the camp boss,' the girl replied. 'He said he was leaving in the morning and would be on the trail for maybe a week. I guess he took it in. He can only be making for the Ross place, and Phil Brady is going with him.'

'Just the two of them?' the man demanded.

'That's right. No large party. You'll be able to take him easy.'

'It will never be easy taking Slade Hollister,' the man retorted. 'He killed Ned Bunch the other day, and Ned was no slouch in any class. But you know what will happen if you try to trick us, Charlie. Drogo will take you himself, and I wouldn't want to be around to see what he'd do to you.'

'Me and Grandpa told Rolph we'd play it like he said,' the girl protested. 'Slade thinks we're on the level. I'll be watching him until he rides out to check if he sends for help or takes more men. If he does I'll get word to you.'

Slade drew his gun, easing forward as he did so. He saw the man moving away from the girl and cocked his gun, the clicks loud and ominous in the silence. The man turned instantly, reaching for his holstered gun.

'Don't try it,' Slade warned. 'You're covered.'

'Hollister.' The man froze, his hands moving outwards away from his waist. 'Charlie, you double-crossed us.'

'No.' The girl gasped. 'I told Rolph that Hollister was too smart for him. He didn't fall for our story after all.' She turned and started running towards the Riley wagon.

Slade let her go. He watched his man carefully. 'All right,' he said. 'Turn around so I can take your gun, and just remember who I am. I don't want to kill you, mister. I need you for a talk, but I'll drop you in your tracks if you try to get smart.'

The man made no reply and turned slowly. Slade closed in and secured the holstered gun. Then he pushed the man forward.

'Over to that coach,' he said. 'I want to take a look at you, and hear what you got to say for yourself.'

They crossed to Becker's coach and entered. Becker looked up in surprise, and Slade told the camp boss what he had overheard as he watched his man. He had never seen the man before, but figured him to be one of Rolph's new men. When questioned, the man refused to give his name or state his business.

'Hold him here, Chain, until I get back,' Slade said. 'I have a couple more people to get hold of.'

Becker pulled a gun and menaced the prisoner, and Slade left the coach and went across to the Riley wagon. Charlie and Banjo were in a hurry to harness their horses, and Slade called to them from the shadows.

'It's no use trying to run for it,' he told them. 'You're in trouble and I want to talk to you.'

The old man swung around, reaching for the gun holstered on his hip, and Slade clenched his teeth.

'Don't be a fool, Banjo,' he snapped. 'I've got my gun on you.'

Slade waited until the old man's gun had cleared leather. He was moving forwards, trying to get to close quarters, but he was still a good ten feet away when Banjo started levelling his big sixgun. Cursing, Slade thumbed off a shot that sent a string of echoes thundering through the darkened camp, and the orange muzzle flash of his .45 lanced through the shadows. Banjo Riley flung down his gun and twisted sharply, falling limply to the ground, and as the noise of the shot faded Charlene Riley stood screaming as if she would never stop.

Men came running, and lanterns threw yellow glare upon the scene. Slade dropped to one knee beside the oldster, and Banjo's eyes glinted in the light.

'Slade, don't hold it against me,' he said brokenly. 'Rolph got a hold over me. I had to do it. But Charlie wasn't mixed up in it. Do what you can for that gal, huh?'

Slade thinned his lips, and before he could make any reply the old man was dead. He got to his feet, a heavy sigh tearing from him, and he went to the sobbing girl. When he put a hand upon her shoulder she jerked away, reviling him, and he grasped her firmly, slapping her face sharply to bring her out of the shock that gripped her distraught mind. The next moment a heavy hand grasped his left shoulder, cruel fingers digging into the wound he had taken there from Ned Bunch. Swinging around, he found himself confronted by Frank Burden.

'What the hell is going on here, Hollister?' Burden demanded.

'Railroad business,' Slade retorted. 'Don't get in my hair, Burden. I've got a lot to do.'

'Did you kill old Banjo?'

'He was pulling his gun on me. I'll make a report to you later.' Slade was only too aware of the men beginning to crowd around, and Phil Brady was one of the foremost.

'Banjo pulled a gun on you?' Burden demanded heavily. 'Who are you kidding? I've known that harmless old man for thirty years.

'I said I'll report you later, when I've finished my inquiries,' Slade said. 'Now stand aside.'

'Oh no!' There was deep satisfaction in Burden's harsh tones. 'I've had about all I can take from you, Hollister. You figured to step into your father's boots, but as far as I'm concerned it doesn't work out. I'm suspending you from duty and Brady is taking over. He should have had the promotion instead of you anyhow.'

'I've got one of Drogo Rolph's men in Becker's coach,' Slade said through his teeth. 'He was talking with Charlene here making plans for me to walk into a trap. Now you'd better stand aside, Burden, and let me do what I get paid for. You can't suspend me from duty. If you've got any complaints about the way I'm handling my work then make them to Colonel Bill.'

'That's where you're wrong,' Burden retorted, and now there was a slick grin on his heavy face. 'I've been in touch with the Colonel, explaining about the trouble we've got here, and he's given me the power to act on my own initiative. I'm suspending you from duty until an inquiry can be made into this affair, and in the meantime Phil Brady takes over your job. Put him right about what you have done, then go back to Big Bend and remain there until I contact you.'

For a moment Slade stared into Burden's face, fighting down the impulse to start fighting. But he knew violence would only make matters worse, and he tightened his lips. In the background Phil Brady stood grinning triumphantly, and Slade was tempted to wipe that smile away by telling Burden what he knew about Brady and Lola. But he was aware that such a revelation would not help him or the situation, so he clamped his teeth together and turned away, making for Becker's coach.

Burden followed them into the camp boss's coach, and Slade explained the situation, then stood in the background while Burden and Brady tried to get their prisoner to talk. The man remained sullenly mute, and Charlene was too hysterical to say anything. But it was out of Slade's hands now, and he turned and left them to it. He would catch the next train back to Big Bend.

Slade was in a depressed mood when he left end of track on the work train. Reaching Las Corros, he went into the telegraph office and asked for any wires. There was nothing, and he caught the next train through to Big Bend. His spirits rose a little when he found Hard Sam waiting at the depot for him, but his father's face was grim, and Slade wondered what else had gone wrong.

'I guess you've heard about me, huh?' Slade demanded.

Sam nodded slowly as he studied Slade's face. 'I got a wire from Burden telling me to forget what I'm doing here helping you and to get the hell out of it because you're suspended and Brady is handling operations now. I heard you killed old Banjo Riley, and I figure you had good cause to. Burden is claiming you lost your head, but I trained you different to that, son. Let's go have a beer, huh? Then you can relax and tell me whatever you've got on your mind.'

'Okay. I got nothing better to do.' Slade kept his tone level, although he was low in spirits.

They went into the Silver Concho and bought two beers, moving to a table where they could talk out of earshot of the tender behind the bar. Sam sipped his beer, thoughtful for a moment, and then he leaned forwards and spoke in an undertone.

Don't worry about what Burden and Brady will do, Slade,' he confided. 'I've already put our plan into action. I'm passing on false information about non-existent gold shipments to the various men who could be working in with Rolph. We'll know in a week or so if there's anything to it.'

'A week or two.' Dismay sounded in Slade's tones, and Sam grinned.

'Don't be so impatient, son.' He spoke sharply despite his smile. 'The first thing you've got to learn in this business when you're bossing it is that you can't do everything at once. Take it easy. So you've been suspended. Okay, sit back and have a rest. Burden and Brady have taken over. That's good. I figure they'll both show themselves up for the fools they are. I never did figure Phil Brady as any good for bossing the outfit. Now why don't you go let the Doc look you over, then turn in for a couple of days? You look like you could sleep for a week. I'll handle this side of it, and watch out for your interests. If anything comes out of this trap we're setting I'll put you onto it, and you'll get the credit. It'll show Burden and Brady up for what they are.'

Slade nodded slowly. He felt as if he had reached the end of his rope both mentally and physically, and when he finished his beer he left the saloon and went along to the Doc's place. His wounds were tended and he received the same advice that Hard Sam had given him. He had to rest up. Since there was nothing else he could do he went home and stripped for bed. He lay for a long time thinking over the situation, reliving the tough incident that had occurred, trying to puzzle out who could be passing information to Drogo Rolph, and it seemed that his only hope of successfully breaking the deadlock lay in Hard Sam's trap working. He closed his eyes and fell into a dreamless sleep.

CHAPTER TWELVE

In the week that followed, Slade rarely left the house. He sat around, low spirited, thoughtful, concerned about his future and the way his job was being handled by Phil Brady. Each successively monotonous day added to his despair, and even Hard Sam was unable to change his attitude. Three times during that week Sam reported on his ruse to get the unknown informant to reveal himself, but each effort with a non-existent gold shipment brought no reaction and failed to expose the guilty man.

'I don't think this trap of yours is gonna spring on anyone, Sam,' Slade said one evening when he and his father were in the saloon having a quiet drink. It was now two weeks after Slade had been suspended by Frank Burden, and Burden had not spoken to Slade on the few occasions when they came into contact. Brady had not shown up in Big Bend since Slade's suspension and there was no news of Brady's activities. But Drogo Rolph had not been taken. 'I figure our man is too smart to get taken in. He must be aware that you're passing on fake information.'

'I reckon you've got something there,' Sam said harshly. 'Maybe I'd better try a different angle.'

'Such as?' Slade sounded hopeless.

'I've been using fake information. Maybe I ought to try the opposite. If I use real information, but have it kept from everyone but the man we are testing, then we might get some results. I can arrange that with Colonel Bill. You know he's angry about the way Burden suspended you, but he told me he can't step in to do anything about it without causing even more trouble. He thinks like I do, that Brady will make a hash of this and you will be reinstated.'

'I'm getting tired of sitting around doing nothing but thinking about the situation,' Slade said. 'You go ahead with what you're trying, Sam. It seems to me it's the only thing we do have going for us right now. I'm gonna take a trip to Jules

Crossing. I want to check up on that gal who got hurt in the shooting there, and find out what's become of Flash Dan Delmont. If you want me for anything then contact me there. I'll hop the freight out in an hour and pick up a horse in Las Corros. I can ride the train to end of track and push on from there.'

'Sure, son,' Hard Sam said quietly. 'I figure a trip will do you good. But keep in touch. I'm gonna try and save time now. Colonel Bill changed his mind about dragging me away pronto. He reckons I better stick around here until this situation has been resolved. But even he will have a time limit, and I figure I'm getting mighty close to the end of it. The two men I've been keeping till last to test are Burden and Phil Brady. I reckon it will be easy for me to work it so only the two of them have advance knowledge of the next big gold shipment. If anything happens we shall at least know one of them is the guilty man. But you get away from Big Bend for a few days. I'll contact you at Jules Crossing if anything comes up.'

At Las Corros Slade picked up a Company horse from the stable and put it aboard the work train leaving soon for end of track, and he was aboard the train when it pulled out. It was dawn when they reached the construction camp, and Slade de-trained his mount and prepared to ride out. Before he left the camp he looked up Chain Becker, who was at the end of track supervising the day's work. Becker grinned at sight of him.

'Glad to see you, Slade,' he said, moving to one side to talk. 'Have you got your job back? Brady has been running around in circles, I can tell you, trying to fill your boots as well as your job, and I heard that Marshal McCall over in Jules Crossing practically kicked him out of town because of the way he's been trying to get a lead on the outlaws from the prisoners McCall has got.'

'I'm on my way to Jules Crossing now,' Slade said. 'I got some unfinished business there. I am still suspended, and I figure Burden means to give Brady his chance. What happened about that outlaw I picked up when I had to kill Banjo Riley? Didn't they get anything out of him?'

'Not that I know of. They took him to the jail in Jules Crossing and he's being held there.'

'That's good, Chain. I'll see you later. I'm riding on now. I want to be in Jules Crossing early.'

'Watch your step then,' Becker said. 'Charlene Riley has been talking up trouble for you. She reckons to get a couple of men to bushwhack you someplace for killing old Banjo.'

'So that's the way it goes,' Slade said, and went to his mount and swung into the saddle, riding away at a canter, following the surveyor's markers to Jules Crossing. Five miles ahead of end of track he came across the graders and engineers, preparing the ground for the tracks, and he continued without stopping.

When he reached Jules Crossing he rode along the street to the law office, dismounting and entering, pausing on the threshold to wipe sweat from his forehead. Jake McCall was at the desk, and the town marshal got to his feet and came forwards to shake hands.

Glad to see you, Slade,' the lawman said. 'You're looking a lot better than when I saw you last. Got your job back yet?'

'Nope, and I'm okay now. Two weeks sitting around has healed my flesh, but it ain't done much for my mind. How's it going here?'

'I got a case against Trimble that will keep him out of circulation for quite a time. You'll be needed at the trial, Slade, but that won't be for weeks yet.'

'What about the outlaw from Rolph's gang? Has he had anything to say about anything that might interest me?'

'Nope. He's closemouthed. Brady was here yesterday, and I got to hold his prisoner for a while longer.'

'How's Maisie? I heard she's gonna live.'

'She's over at the hotel, and she said for me to tell you she wants to see you when you show up. I told her you was fixing to pay her bills while she's unable to work.'

'Who do I pay?' Slade demanded.

'The Doc said he'd see you when you came back, and the hotel are taking care of Maisie until you get around to them.'

'Okay, Jake. I'll check with you again before I ride out. I want to have a talk with Maisie. I figure she does know where Drogo Rolph might be, but up till now she wasn't talking. Now she might change her mind. But before I go, what happened to Flash Dan Delmont and his hardcases?'

'He pulled out of town soon as he got out of jail. I reckon he found it too tough for his business around here. I've heard nothing of him since he left.'

Slade left the office. He swung into his saddle and rode to the stable, leaving the horse in the care of the stableman. Then he went along to the hotel. The doctor was in the lobby, talking to the clerk. Slade smiled as he approached them.

'I was coming to see you about Maisie, Doc,' he said. 'How is she doing?'

'She's up now, but it'll be a few weeks before she'll be fully recovered,' the medico replied. 'She was lucky, Slade. For a time her chances were less than fifty-fifty.'

'Which room is she in?'

'Don't get tough with her,' the clerk said. 'Phil Brady went to work on her when he was here the day before yesterday, and I figured it did her a lot of harm.'

'Brady?' Slade's face hardened. 'I haven't come here to make it tough for Maisie. If Brady got out of line with her I'll take it up with him later.'

The clerk told him which room the girl was in and Slade went up the stairs, pausing for a moment at the door of the room. Then he knocked gently. When the girl's voice answered from inside it sounded nervous and hesitant.

'This is Slade Hollister, Maisie,' he said. 'You don't have to be afraid of me.'

There was the sound of the door being unbolted. Then it opened a crack and Maisie Clapham's pallid face peered out at him. The girl sighed with relief and opened the door wide, smiling now. But there were signs of strain in her features.

'I was afraid it was Phil Brady again, Hollister,' she said. 'He gave me a rough time a couple of days ago. He figured I knew where Drogo Rolph is hiding out.'

'I'll twist his neck when I see him again,' Slade said heavily. 'How you feeling now, Maisie? You were in a bad way a couple of weeks ago.'

'I'm on my feet, but I can't do anything except sit around. I'm still pretty weak. But the Doc says I'm lucky. That was a tough night, huh?'

'I was a lot luckier than you!' Slade said. 'I walked away from the shooting.'

'Doc said you got hit three times.'

'Yeah, but none serious. Jake McCall said you wanted to see me. What can I do for you?'

'The marshal said you told him you'd pick up my bills until I'm on my feet again,' Maisie said, and her pale face tightened. 'I don't have any dough, Hollister, but I don't want you to feel obliged to help me.'

'You wouldn't have been shot if I hadn't got you across to the jail,' he retorted. 'Don't worry about a thing, Maisie.' He reached into his breast pocket and produced a roll of bills, peeling off five twenties. He laid the money on a table, watching her face expressing protest as she saw how much he was giving her. 'A hundred bucks,' he said. 'That should hold you for a spell, huh? If you need any more then let me know.'

Tears came to her eyes and her lips tightened. Slade smiled softly.

'Come on, Maisie, there's no need to get worked up about it. There are no strings attached to that dough. I figure you do know where Drogo Rolph might be, but I'm not making any conditions for this money. It's yours and that's an end to it. You just take it easy and rest up, and if that jasper Phil Brady shows up here again then tell him you're under my protection and he'd better see me.'

'Hollister, if you're telling me the truth about that dough, that there's no strings attached, then this is the first time in my life a man has done something for me without expecting to get paid some way for it.' Tears rolled down her cheeks and Hollister thinned his lips.

'Cut it out,' he said gently. 'You have to get a break sometime, Maisie. Maybe this is your turn, huh?'

'I heard you need a break,' she retorted, drying her eyes and looking up into his face with a gleaming blue gaze. 'You lost your job, didn't you? That Phil Brady took over from you. I guess if you picked up Drogo Rolph it would make everything right for you again? Brady would lose out.'

'Do you know where Drogo is hiding out?' he asked, his pulses racing.

'I heard what you did to Banjo Riley. Charlene is out to get you, Hollister.' Maisie was still trying to sound tough. 'She's trying to hire a couple of fast guns to take care of you. Well, I figure I owe you something, and not just because of that hundred bucks. You're doing me a great favour, and from the goodness of your heart. You've made me feel cheap. I reckon I can ease my mind some by doing you a good turn. I'll tell you where Rolph is probably hiding. But I may not be doing you a favour. If you go out there you'll likely get yourself killed.'

'You can leave me to worry about that,' Slade said instantly. 'I'll take my chances. Maisie, if you want to spill the beans.'

'I do.' The girl's tones were firm, her face showing determination. 'Listen, Hollister, I've had time to do a lot of thinking this past week or so. I've made a lot of mistakes in my time, and I met all kinds. There have been too many of Rolph's kind and not enough of yours. Okay, so maybe I can ease my conscience by doing something right for a change. But if you get out to Rolph's place and they catch you and kill you I'd have a bad conscience for the rest of my life.'

'Telling me where to go would give me a better chance than I got now,' he retorted grimly. 'At least I would be able to meet Rolph face to face. The way he's trying for me now, I could collect a bullet in the back at any time.'

'That's right.' She nodded slowly. 'You know Pinto Creek?'

'Sure. I lost Rolph's trail around there more than once.'

'Make for Pinto Creek. Follow the line of hills northeast and hit Rattlesnake Canyon. Through Rattlesnake there's a flat-topped hill.'

'I know it,' Slade said quickly.

'Pass the flat-topped hill on the left and you'll find a game trail. You'll have to look hard for it. That game trail will lead you into a ravine. There's a gully on the left in the ravine. It's overgrown, and they pull a couple of tumbleweeds over their tracks before it to blot them. The gully itself is concealed with brush, but you'll find it if you're looking for it. Go through the gully and you'll find yourself in a box canyon. There's no other way in or out. That's where Drogo and his gang will likely be. Watch out for a guard. They have a man watching the ravine from the top, and he'll pass on the word, if you're spotted, to a second guard in the gully. You'll never get in there if they see you, Hollister, and if you get in there and they catch you then you'll never get out alive.'

'I'm prepared to take my chances,' he answered. 'I've waited a long time to get Drogo Rolph. I won't miss any opportunity now.'

'I'll be around here for some time to come,' she said. 'Look me up again afterwards, huh?'

'I'll do that! You can bet your boots I will, Maisie. And tell Marshal McCall if there's anything you want. He'll take care of it, and let me know later. If Brady bothers you then I'll take care of him, but I'll have a word with McCall about Brady. See you later, Maisie. I got a lot to handle right now.'

'Good luck,' she replied, and her face was hard. 'I hope I'm not sending you to your death, Hollister, after what you've done for me. I hope it works out for you.'

'I'll try and make it,' he assured her as he took his leave.

Going back to the law office, Slade asked McCall to let him talk to the outlaw he had arrested the night Banjo Riley was shot dead, and McCall accompanied him into the cell block. The outlaw was stretched out on his bunk, and Harvey Trimble was being held in the adjoining cell. Trimble got to his feet when he saw Slade, jeering sullenly when Slade passed his door.

'So they dragged you down, huh, Hollister?' the freighter demanded. 'I reckon you'll get your come-uppance yet. You'll pay for what you did to me.'

Slade ignored the man, and Trimble fell silent when McCall threatened to enter the cell and beat him if he did not shut up. Slade looked at the outlaw, recalling the night he had seen the man talking to Charlene Riley.

'On your feet,' McCall snapped angrily, and the outlaw arose, gazing sullenly at Slade.

'You want to get out of here?' Slade demanded without preamble. He saw a flicker in the outlaw's eyes, but McCall protested instantly.

'I can't turn him loose, Slade,' the town marshal said.

'Why not? He's my prisoner. I took him at the end of track. I need him now to get at Drogo Rolph. If he takes me where I want to go I'll turn him loose. If he doesn't play along then he'll come back here and stand trial.'

'What would Brady say if I let you take him?' McCall demanded. 'Hell, you know I'd do anything for you, Slade, and that's the gospel. If you hit me I wouldn't hit you back. But it could cost me my job.'

'Tell Brady or Burden that I came in here claiming to be back in my old job, and if anything goes wrong later I'll back you up in that. But I want this hombre, Jake. He could lead me to Drogo Rolph.'

'Okay, you can have him,' McCall said. He unlocked the cell door and motioned for the outlaw to emerge. The man strode through to the office, turning to face Slade.

'If you figure I'm gonna turn against Rolph and tell you where he is then you're surely wasting your time,' he rasped.

'I don't need you to tell me anything,' Slade retorted. 'I know where Rolph is. All I want you for is to let the guards at the hideout see you in my company. They'll figure I'm with you and we should get in there without trouble. Once inside I'll be ready to start shooting, and I'll put an end to the Drogo Rolph bunch if it's the last thing I do.'

His words startled and silenced the man, and Jake McCall shook his head slowly as he stared into Slade's harshly set face.

'You'll take some help along with you, Slade,' the marshal said.

'No.' Slade shook his head emphatically. 'A bunch of riders would be spotted a mile off. I'm gonna handle this my way. If Brady does show up around here, Jake, warn him off Maisie, huh? I got the urge to twist Brady's neck for what he did to that gal yesterday.'

McCall nodded, sighing heavily, but he showed by his expression that he did not like the idea Slade was working on. Slade took his prisoner and departed, making for the stable, and after they had picked up their mounts they rode onto the store for provisions. Slade knew he had a three-day ride out to the hideout and another three days back, if he ever got out alive, and he had their supplies put in two sacks, tying one behind each cantle of their saddles. They rode out at a canter, the outlaw on Slade's left, and as they left the town behind Slade felt a great weight lift from his mind.

They camped that night, and if the outlaw realized they were on the trail to Rolph's hideout, he said nothing. Slade tied the man and slept lightly, awakening before dawn to prepare breakfast. As they sat and ate, Slade tried to draw the man into conversation.

'There's no point you remaining silent any longer,' Slade said. 'I'm not a lawman, and if you help me get into Rolph's camp then I'll have no further interest in you. You'll be free again. I want Drogo Rolph and I mean to get him.'

'You must be loco,' came the sullen reply. 'If you get into that camp you'll never get out alive.'

'I don't care about that. I'm gonna finish Drogo Rolph, and this is likely the only chance I'll get.'

They rode on, travelling through the heat of the day, and two more days passed before they reached Pinto Creek. Slade reined up in cover and studied the area for a long time, but there were no signs of life and they went on, following the line of hills northeast. There were a lot of hoofprints around, but they did not mean anything, and he found Rattlesnake Canyon, trailing through it with his hand on his gun and his nerves taut, his reflexes hair-triggered. Leaving the canyon, he spotted the flat-crowned hill, and when they passed to its left the silent outlaw glanced speculatively at Slade.

'I'm beginning to believe you have learned where Rolph's hideout is,' he said.

'I was telling you the truth,' Slade retorted. 'Just along here now there's a game trail I got to find, and that'll lead us into a ravine. In the ravine there's a gully. The gully will lead into a box canyon, where the hideout is. There's a guard watching the ravine and another in the gully.' He grinned. 'Doesn't that convince you I know what I'm talking about?'

'What do you want from me?' the man demanded reluctantly.

'You know where the guards are positioned?'

'Sure. But they won't let me ride in there. It's been nearly three weeks since I left Rolph with orders to check on Banjo Riley. They'll figure I either got taken or pulled out for good.'

'What kind of a hold did they have over Banjo?'

'I don't know, but the old man sure was scared of Rolph. Mebbe he was concerned for his daughter.'

'Grand-daughter,' Slade said.

'It's all the same to me.' The outlaw looked around. 'If I get you into the box canyon you'll keep your word and let me ride free?'

'That's the only deal I got to offer you,' Slade replied.

'Okay, I'll take you up on that. But you'll have to ride ahead of me, Hollister. If those guards spot you at my back they'll figure you're holding a gun on me.'

'I can plug you from ahead as easily as from behind,' Slade said. 'I'm just desperate enough to give you this break. Okay, so let's get on and get into that box canyon. Soon as I see it is the right place you can duck out and go where ever you like. I'll be busy trying to take Rolph. But I'll tell you this much. If I ever see you around again I'll pull you in.'

They went on, and the outlaw pointed out the game trail Maisie had mentioned. Slade began to tense, and his right hand was close to the butt of his gun as they continued. When they entered the ravine he looked around for sight of the guard, but saw nothing, and at once he began to fear that Rolph had moved out. Then a man suddenly stood up on the rim of the ravine, a rifle in his hands, and his voice echoed as he called to them.

'Hey there, Bennett. Where in hell you been? Rolph has been going loco because you didn't get back.'

'I had trouble, and then some,' the outlaw responded. 'But it's okay now.'

'Who's that with you?' the guard demanded.

'An old friend of mine. He wants to join up with the outfit.'

'Okay, go on. Watch out for Pierce. He's covering the gully.'

They rode on, and Slade led the way, feeling a tingling sensation along his spine. He kept glancing over his shoulder at his prisoner, and the man seemed happy with the situation.

'You getting worried now, Hollister?' he inquired. 'I figure this is the tightest spot you ever rode into. Whatever you do, I can't see you riding out of this one.'

'You just concentrate on not trying to get smart,' Slade replied in low tones. 'If there is trouble and you put me in a bad light then any shot I manage to get off will be directed at you.'

'It ain't me you got to worry about,' the outlaw remarked.

'It'll be the gang. Whatever you do, don't let yourself be taken alive by Rolph. You killed Ned Bunch, and Rolph ain't ever likely to forget that. He's worse than an Injun when it comes to making a man pay for something he's done. I wouldn't want to be in your saddle for twice the amount of gold Rolph has stolen from your railroad.'

Slade made no reply, and they passed the second guard without seeing him. Then they were entering the box canyon, and Slade reined up instantly, spotting several shacks built beside a creek to the left. He turned to speak to the outlaw, intending to tell the man to get out while he could, but as he swung around in his saddle the second guard appeared from behind a rock, and there was a levelled rifle in his hands. Slade jumped his bronc sideways, pulling his sixgun as he did so, and then the crash of shots blasted out the silence, sending echoes crashing away across the canyon.

CHAPTER THIRTEEN

The guard's first shot skimmed Slade's head as his mount cavorted at the gunfire. Slade ducked slightly, his right hand swinging forward his long-barrelled Colt. He fired instinctively, aiming roughly, intent upon downing his man and then moving in against the gang before they could recover from their surprise. His bullet hit the man's rifle, and the weapon was whirled out of the guard's hand. The man reached for his holstered sixgun, and Slade crinkled his eyes against the gunsmoke and sent a bullet into the centre of the man's chest. Slade looked round as his man went down in a heap. His prisoner was riding away back along the gully.

Spurring his horse, Slade went across to the shacks, and already there was a man standing in front of one of them, holding a rifle and preparing to use it. Slade started shooting, his gun swinging easily.

The man in front of the shack went down bending at the knees and waist like a man who is dead before he hits the ground. A door was jerked open in another shack and a man appeared, sixgun in hand. Slade ducked in his saddle as lead came for him, and squeezed off a shot that took the man about waist high. The hammering blasts of Colt-fire boomed echoingly across the canyon.

Sunlight glittered on the flat surface of a pool to the left, and Slade narrowed his eyes against the glare, catching a glimpse of movement in that direction. He saw a man running from the water, naked, his body gleaming in the sunlight, and as the bather bent to snatch up a gun from his pile of clothing, Slade sent a bullet through him.

Swinging his horse, Slade went between two of the shacks. Drawing a sharp breath, he dismounted and moved to the rear of the nearest shack. He had surprise on his side and he meant to take advantage of it. He reached a window in the side of the shack, which was glassless, and thrust his head and gunhand inside, looking for a target. The shack was empty and he spun on his heel and went to the next. Gun echoes still clung to the sunlight air in the canyon, muttering and grumbling reluctantly away in the distance.

Slade burst in a door and blundered into the next shack, his gun ready to continue the fight, but it, too, was empty, and he paused for breath, peering around, moving to a window to check what was happening outside. There were two more shacks to be searched, and no movement showed anywhere around them. The echoes were fading now and he began to realize the truth. Drogo Rolph's gang was not here in strength.

Going to check his victims, he found they were all the newer members of Rolph's gang. Rolph himself was absent, and so were Mulie Johnson and Bull Seymour. Slade stood by the creek wondering about it. Where was Rolph? Had he gone out on another job?

Fetching his horse, Slade rode back to the gully, on the watch for his prisoner and more trouble. He checked the dead guard, finding the man's pistol and rifle gone, and he was aware that his prisoner had taken the risk to come back for the weapons. The man was now armed, and there was also a guard in the ravine between Slade and open country.

He rode with his rifle in his right hand, the barrel resting across his thighs. His pale eyes glinted as he stared around, and his blood still raced from the shooting that had taken place. A rifle cracked and he heard the bullet sing past his right ear. He was in the ravine and there was no room for manoeuvre. Hunching his shoulders, he rode as fast as the rough ground would permit, and two more shots hammered out the silence before he hit the exit and lost himself to view. There was sweat on his forehead as he reined up and took stock of his surroundings. In the distance a rider was making off to the west. The flat-topped hill was just before him.

Slade knew he had to cut his losses and return to Jules Crossing. He set his face in the required direction and rode steadily, intent upon having a further talk with Maisie. The girl might know of other hideouts where Rolph could be.

Three days later he sighted the town, and it was in the middle of the afternoon when he hit the main street. The sun was baking the dusty street, and Jules Crossing appeared to be sleeping through the heat. Entering the stable, Slade took care of his horse, then shouldered his saddlebags and took hold of his rifle. He left the stable, intending to make his way to the law office, but as he reached the sidewalk Charlene Riley appeared from an alley opposite. There was a man with her.

Slade saw the girl immediately, and knew trouble was upon him, but he did not halt, knowing that a moving target was much harder to hit. He lifted his rifle as he moved, watching the man beside the girl, and as the man reached for his holstered sixgun, Slade dropped to one knee and threw up his rifle.

The town seemed to cringe to the gunblasts, and Slade realized that he was being fired at from two different directions. The man with Charlene was working his sixgun, but there was an extra gun somewhere, throwing lead. He felt a burning pain across the left side of his head, just above the ear, and his hat went sailing off his head. He saw Charlene lifting a sixgun to join in against him, but he was concentrating upon the man, and he got up and started moving to cover when the man suddenly dropped his gun, clutched at his chest and pitched sideways against the girl.

A rifle was still shooting from along the street, and Slade, reaching an alley, ducked into cover and then turned to check on the situation. The rifle was not firing at him. It was shooting from a window of the hotel, and its slugs were hammering into the doorway of the saloon across the street. In the background Jake McCall was moving steadily along the sidewalk, and it seemed that he knew the identity of the rifleman in the hotel because he was in the open and ignoring the fire. Slade moved out of cover, and Charlene Riley cut loose at him with a pistol. A bullet crackled past Slade's head, and he swung angrily and sent three quick shots at the girl, none of them intended to hit her. He saw her drop the pistol and turn to run into cover, and he clenched his teeth and went on, a frown on his forehead.

The rifle ceased firing from the hotel as McCall reached the saloon, and the marshal thrust through the batwings and disappeared from sight. A moment later, as Slade was moving forward to check, McCall reappeared, and there was a man preceding him, his hands in the air. The town marshal was grinning tightly, ordering his prisoner to halt, and they waited for Slade to reach them.

'You got Maisie to thank for your life, Slade,' the town marshal said. 'She's been sitting at her window overlooking the street with a rifle for days now, waiting for you to ride in. I got wind that Charlene Riley was waiting with two hardcases for you to return, and Maisie was looking out for you. She kept this hombre off your neck while you shot it out with the other. Did you hit Charlene?'

'No. I scared her off.'

'How'd you make out with your business?' McCall was glancing around the street.

'I nailed some of them, but not the ones I wanted. Have there been any calls for me from Big Bend?'

'I'll say there has. You better get down to the telegraph office right away. There must be a stack of wires for you a mile high.'

'Okay. I'll check with you later.' Slade turned and went fast along the sidewalk to the telegraph office.

'You've been in great demand for almost a week, Slade, the number of wires that came for you. McCall told me to hold them for you, figuring you'd be back.' The telegraph operator turned at sight of Slade and picked up a sheaf of wires. 'The latest ones are on top, and things have been humming while you've been away.'

Slade took the wires and hastily scanned the top one. Drogo Rolph had hit another train, escaping with thirty thousand dollars. Hard Sam had given up his trick to get the renegade railroad man to expose his hand and had leaked information of real gold shipments to some of the men he suspected, taking them singly, working through the list, and scoring no success until he had informed Burden and Phil Brady of a shipment. That shipment had been stolen by Drogo Rolph. Burden had been confronted by Hard Sam, and denied any complicity with the gang. Phil Brady had disappeared on the trail and had not been heard of for several days. Slade had been reinstated as chief troubleshooter and had to report at Big Bend as soon as possible.

Slade found his senses whirling with the revelations, and he sent a wire to Hard Sam, informing his father of his activities and intentions. He would be returning to Big Bend immediately. Leaving the telegraph office, Slade went along the sidewalk to the hotel, and Maisie was there, her face showing anxiety, hope, and fear.

'I can't stop to talk to you, Maisie,' Slade said. 'I've got to ride out at once. But I hit the gang in the hideout.' He explained what had happened, and saw the girl's fear deepen when she learned that Rolph had not been taken.

'Don't worry about it. Just stay put here and I'll come back and see you later.' Slade was in a hurry. 'I've got time to get some food, then I must ride. There's hell to pay for what's been happening.'

McCall came to him while he was eating in the restaurant, and the town marshal was grim when he learned all the news.

'But at least you got your job back, huh?' he said. 'What's happened to Brady?'

'Probably took out after Rolph after the robbery. He'll show up sometime, and maybe he's got some questions to answer when I do see him. I'm riding out almost at once, Jake. I got to be back in Big Bend soon as possible.'

'Okay. I don't have to answer to you for that prisoner you took out of my jail and lost, huh?'

'No. I let him go, but I got some of his pards. What about Charlene Riley?'

'I just picked her up. I'll let her cool off in jail for a few days.'

'Don't be too hard on her. I did kill Banjo.'

'The way I heard it you had to. She oughta known better than to mix up with outlaws.' There was a rough note in McCall's voice.

Slade pushed the horse as he rode out. He had been working at full stretch for almost a week now and his nights had been short and practically sleepless. His trip out and back in search of Rolph had taken the fine edge from his alertness, but he was in a dangerous frame of mind, ready to jump and fight at the drop of a hat.

It was full dark when he passed the camp where the graders were working, and he continued to end of track, arriving in Becker's camp just before midnight. He turned his horse into the corral and went along to Becker's coach, frowning when he spotted lights across the darkened camp and heard the sound of music coming through the shadows. There was a light in Becker's office, and Slade tapped at the door and entered. Chain Becker looked up from his bookwork, then grinned and got to his feet.

'Am I glad to see you, Slade.' He said. 'I've got trouble again. Flash Dan is back with another tented saloon.'

'Is that his place I saw across the camp?' Slade demanded.

'That's it, and a lot of my men are in it. I've had as much trouble as the last time. Work is being affected and schedules are getting behind. The workers have asked for a wage handout so they can drink and gamble. I wired Hard Sam and he's sending a payroll through soon as he can. But he's got no one to guard it. Brady hasn't been seen since he took out after Drogo Rolph after the last robbery. You heard about that, I suppose.'

'Yeah, I heard. Now what am I to do about Delmont? Burden didn't like it that last time I took care of him.'

'I was told by Hard Sam to lay off until you arrived. I heard some time ago you had showed up again in Jules Crossing. Sam said you've got to handle the chore, Slade.'

'You got any men around here you can trust?' Slade demanded.

'Sure, about a score. You want to tear that saloon down like we planned the last time?' Becker's eyes began to glitter. 'I got some excess energy I'd like to waste away in that saloon, and I'd sure like to connect with Flash Dan's smooth jaw.'

'I reckon they'll be expecting that,' Slade said, 'and some of your men might get hurt. I don't figure you'll get much more trouble until the payroll turns up here, huh?'

'That's a fact.'

'Well I figure to leave Delmont until I get back. I must go on to Las Corros, Chain. You got an engine handy?'

'Sure.' Becker grinned. 'I told you I heard you was on your way here from Jules Crossing. I delayed the work train so you could ride it. You'll find it out there waiting to move off. See you when you get back. And I'm sure glad you got your job back.'

Slade departed, and went to the waiting work train. He spoke with the driver then climbed onto a flat car, spreading his

115

blankets in the darkness and lying down to rest. He was asleep until the train reached Las Corros. There he transferred to the through train, and at dawn he stepped off the passenger coach onto the platform in Big Bend.

The sun was barely peeping over the eastern horizon when Slade left the depot and made his way to the house he shared with his father. But he was disappointed when he found the house empty. Sam was away. He made breakfast, then cleaned up and changed into a suit, feeling civilized once more, and his sixgun was dust-free and gleaming when he buckled his heavy cartridge belt around his waist and tied down the holster.

He went back to the depot to see Frank Burden, not relishing a meeting with the Area Manager, but he had to know what was going on and Burden was the only man who could tell him. He entered Burden's office, and was surprised when he discovered it was empty. Frank Burden was always at his desk at this time of the morning. He went on to the telegraph office, and the operator was sitting at his table, eating his breakfast.

'Anything for me?' Slade demanded, and the operator got to his feet.

'Sure is,' he replied, chewing steadily as he moved to a wire basket and took up some message forms. 'Hard Sam has been getting frantic about you. I figure he's sent wires to every rail depot within five hundred miles.'

'Where is Sam?' Slade demanded.

'San Blanca. Gone there to collect the payroll for end of track on the spur between Las Corros and Jules Crossing. Seems those railroad workers want their back pay mighty urgent. You got to be at end of track when the paytrain gets there and watch the payroll until it's been paid to the workers.'

Slade learned from the wires that his father planned to organize a posse in San Blanca and take out on the trail of Drogo Rolph, hoping that the gang boss would make a mistake in his trail blotting and leave some indication of his general direction. Slade smiled grimly as he read the news, for his own experiences at tracking Rolph had always ended in failure. There was nothing else for him, and he tightened his lips when he reckoned that he had to return to end of track when he had just arrived from there.

'Has Phil Brady showed up since the last Rolph robbery?' Slade asked the operator, and the man shook his head.

'He ain't called in neither. Burden was real worried about that last night. Figures Brady caught up with the gang and was killed for his trouble.'

'Where is Frank Burden? He ain't in his office. I just looked. I never known him to be away at this time of the day.'

'Frank got called to El Paso yesterday. He's got trouble on his plate. Seems like only a couple of men knew about the gold shipment Rolph lifted, and one of those two must have passed on the information to the outlaw.'

'Burden and Brady,' Slade said tightly, thinking of Hard Sam's ruse to get the renegade railroader to show his hand. 'And Brady ain't been seen since the robbery. I wonder where in hell he is. I reckon I better start back for Las Corros. If I catch the next through train I should reach there about the time the payroll gets there from San Blanca. But before that dough is paid out to the men I'm gonna make sure there's nothing at end of track for them to spend it on.'

'I heard Flash Dan Delmont was back. You got to watch your step around him this time, Slade. He's gonna be ready for you.'

'He's not the only one.' Slade retorted.

He went to the door and stood for a moment peering out across the tracks, wondering about the situation as always, and his thoughts seemed to have found a rut that led nowhere. Then a thought struck him and he glanced back at the telegraph operator.

'Did Burden take his wife with him when he left for El Paso?' he demanded.

'Don't figure so. Those two had the hell of a bust-up in Las Corros and at end of track, as you know, and they ain't been on speaking terms since. Frank was alone when he got on the train yesterday.'

'When you expecting him back?'

'Can't say. Don't know what will happen to him in El Paso. I guess it's up to Colonel Bill, huh?'

'I guess so.' Slade departed, then turned back. 'You know what I've got to do,' he said. 'When I leave on the train I'll be making for Las Corros, then end of track. If anything urgent crops up you can wire ahead and get them to stop the train and call me.'

'That's what I'll do right enough,' the operator replied.

Slade went along the street to Frank Burden's house. He knocked at the door but there was no reply. The shades were drawn at all the windows and he wondered idly if Lola was alone inside.

When he figured that perhaps Phil Brady was lying low with the woman his eyes glinted and he walked around the house, checking on the windows and the kitchen door. The kitchen door was unlocked and he entered noiselessly, moving through the house, his eyes slitted and his hands clenched. There was a heavy silence inside, and the atmosphere was oppressive. It seemed that the windows had been closed for days on end.

Slade began to look in the rooms, and when he discovered no one on the ground floor he ascended the stairs and looked into the bedrooms. Opening the door of the bedroom overlooking the front of the house he saw Lola asleep in the bed. He paused, undecided, and then he crossed to the bed and bent over the woman, reaching out to shake her.

'Lola, wake up. I got to talk to you,' he said sharply, and she moaned a little before her senses returned. Then her eyes opened and she looked up at him, filled with alarm.

'What are you doing here?' she demanded. 'Frank would be pleased to walk in now, huh?'

'That would suit you, wouldn't it?' he countered harshly. 'You wanted me to kill him.'

'No.' She shook her head. 'I wanted Frank moved out of this area, that's all.'

'You know what I think?' he said, standing at the foot of the bed. 'I believe you knew Frank was passing on information about the gold shipments to Rolph. That's why you married him. You reckoned Frank was a stepping stone to a lot of money.'

'Frank never sold information to anyone. You know him better than that, Slade.'

'I figured I knew him quite well, but he sure changed a lot after he married you. Why did you torture him with other men, Lola? You didn't have to marry him and ruin his life. He never was the kind of man you would go for.'

She smiled, and Slade shook his head.

'You know why Frank has gone to El Paso? Do you know Hard Sam has been laying traps for weeks now, trying to get the renegade to show his hand? It finally happened on that last raid Drogo Rolph pulled. Only two men knew about the gold being on that train. That was how it was worked. Frank was one and Brady was the other. Brady ain't been seen since that robbery. I figure he got on Rolph's tracks, pushed too close and was spotted. I figure he's dead now.' He paused, watching her face closely. 'Unless Brady was the informant and he's lying low now with his share of the robberies, waiting for you to join him somewhere.'

'You're a fool, Slade, and you missed some good opportunities when you turned me down. I could have done a lot for you.'

'You did too much as it was,' he said. 'You turned Frank against me. I came close to killing him, but it was the knowledge that you wanted him dead that held me back. I wouldn't give you the satisfaction. You're married to Frank and that is how it'll stay as far as I'm concerned.'

'Why did you come in here?' she demanded. 'What do you think Frank will do if I tell him you broke into the house at this time of the morning?'

'The back door was unlocked,' he said. 'I figure whoever was here last night with you left that way around dawn, huh? Who you got on a string now Brady is gone, Lola?'

'You'd better get out of here,' she snapped. 'If I do tell Frank about it, you coming in here, you'll have to kill him to stay alive.'

'Don't worry, I'm leaving.' He turned to the door. 'I've got to go back to end of track. There's a payroll train pulling in there from San Blanca, and I got to put Flash Dan Delmont out of business before the men can get hold of their money.'

'Is that a fact?' she demanded heavily. 'Well don't let me delay you. Have a nice trip.'

Slade departed, and when he reached the street he took a deep breath to rid himself of the taint of the oppressive atmosphere that had seemed to occupy Frank Burden's house. He went back to the rail depot and talked with the telegraph operator to kill time. Eventually the through train arrived and he boarded it, but he could not relax as he began the trip to Las Corros.

The train pulled out of Big Bend. Slade stared idly from the window. When they hit a gradient and lost speed he spotted a movement beside the track, and twisted in his seat, frowning when he saw a man rise from cover and reach out to swing himself aboard the observation platform at the rear of the last car.

The next moment he was stiffening, coming to full alertness, for he recognized the man without trouble. It was Bull Seymour, one of Drogo Rolph's old gang members.

CHAPTER FOURTEEN

For a moment Slade sat frozen while his brain thrust up a stream of questions about Seymour's presence. Then he got to his feet, his face grim, and walked down the passenger car to the end, leaving it and entering the baggage car. The conductor was sitting at a desk, working over some papers, and he merely glanced up as Slade passed through, making for the observation platform at the rear. Slade loosened his gun in its holster, and before he reached the door that led out to the observation platform he saw it beginning to open slowly. He pulled his gun and moved to the left, letting the opening door shield him. He cocked his gun.

The next moment Bull Seymour came through the doorway, a tall, massively built man dressed in dusty range clothes. He was wearing two pistols holstered in crossed cartridge belts sagging on his big hips, and when he spotted the conductor at his desk he reached for his right hand gun, moving forward a couple of steps. Slade kicked the door shut then, his gun pointing at the bigger man's midriff. Bull Seymour looked around quickly, then froze, his face showing incredulity at sight of Slade covering him.

'Where in hell did you come from?' the big outlaw demanded in booming tones.

'Never mind that,' Slade retorted. 'What are you doing aboard this train and what was your business in Big Bend?'

The outlaw shook his head, his dark eyes narrowed and filled with calculation. Slade smiled grimly.

'I wouldn't try it if I were in your boots, Seymour.'

The conductor was coming forward, exclaiming at the sight of Slade's drawn gun.

'Hold it, Silas.' Slade spoke sharply. 'This is Bull Seymour, one of Drogo's boys. Stay back. Seymour, turn around and get rid of your gunbelts. Just remember that I'd like an excuse to put a slug through you. Tie his feet together, Silas,' Slade continued. 'But leave his hands free.' He kept the outlaw covered, not daring to relax his vigilance until Seymour was helpless. Then he holstered his gun and sat down on a crate several feet away. 'Okay, Bull, now suppose you do some talking?' he said.

'I got nothing to say to you.'

'Well please yourself. I reckon I know a great deal about the gang now. Its days are numbered. Ned Bunch is dead, and that leaves only Drogo himself and Mulie Johnson out of the old gang. Did you know I nailed the other members of the gang a few days ago out at the hideout beyond Pinto Creek?'

Seymour's face was bleak, and Slade grinned. But he was concerned by the big outlaw's presence on the train. When he realized that Seymour would not divulge any information he bound the man's hands securely and left him in the charge of the conductor.

'Keep a gun handy, Silas,' Slade warned. 'I'd better check through the train for any of the others in the gang. They could be aboard. They might be after me.'

He left the baggage car and started a search, but he found no one he knew to be connected with the gang, and relief filled him as he returned to the baggage car. He spent the rest of the trip to Las Corros guarding his prisoner. When they arrived at the town he untied Seymour's feet and took the man off the train, leading him along the street to the law office.

Hart Loman, the town marshal, was at his desk in the office, and he got quickly to his feet at the entrance of Slade and his prisoner, his heavy face showing amazement.

'Hell, ain't that Bull Seymour, Slade?' he demanded.

'It sure is, large as life and twice as nasty. I want to leave him in your jail for a couple of days, Hart.'

'Anything to oblige, but it could get nasty if Rolph learns I got him here.'

'Hire a couple of special deputies,' Slade said. 'The railroad will pay their expenses. I don't want to have to worry about Seymour for the next day or so. I've got a lot to do. There's more trouble at end of track, and a payroll train is due through here from San Blanca at any time, if I haven't already missed it.'

Bull Seymour chuckled harshly at the mention of the payroll

train, and Slade narrowed his eyes as he took in the big outlaw's manner.

'What do you know about that payroll, Seymour?' he demanded.

'Not much, except that it won't reach end of track,' came the grim reply.

Slade turned to the door. He glanced back at Hart Loman.

'Lock him up, Hart, and don't take any chances with him. I'll have him taken to Big Bend soon as I can get round to it.'

He left the office and hurried back to the railroad depot, making for the telegraph office. The operator looked relieved to see him, and picked up a couple of messages from a tray.

'Saw you taking that outlaw in and figured not to detain you until he was under lock and key,' the operator said. 'But there are a couple of messages for you, Slade.'

Slade took the flimsies and looked at them. He was surprised to find one from Frank Burden, telling him that the Area Manager would meet him at Las Corros that night, ordering him to be there waiting. Slade sighed as he looked at the second message, expecting it to be from Hard Sam, but again he was surprised, for it was from Phil Brady. It was terse and to the point. Brady had wired Big Bend, learned of the payroll train going to end of track from San Blanca, and would join the train at Medicine Gulch in order to guard the payroll. He had been trailing Drogo Rolph but lost the outlaws in the hills and was making his way back to Area Headquarters.

'Trouble?' the operator queried.

'I don't know.' Slade shook his head. 'Has the payroll train come through from San Blanca yet? I want to board it and go on to end of track.'

'You're too late. It went through an hour ago.'

'Hell! Did it stop?'

'No.' The operator shook his head. 'I'm expecting telegraph clearance from its next scheduled stop, which is Osage Junction.'

'When is the next train through to end of track?' Slade demanded.

'It'll be the one Frank Burden gets off. You've got to be here to meet him, huh? You can travel together.' The operator

grinned, having heard about the fight that had taken place between Slade and Burden.

'I'll look forward to that,' Slade said heavily.

The telegraph operator called Slade while he was pacing the
platform, and Slade, peering along the line for sight of the train
he wanted, saw a smudge of smoke in the far distance. He
crossed to the operator's side.

'Message from Hard Sam,' the man said, thrusting a paper
into Slade's hand.

Slade read the scribbled message. His father was on his way
to end of track with a posse. Rolph had been seen in Jules
Crossing, Jake McCall had reported, asking for Maisie Clapham. The girl had left Jules Crossing before Rolph had shown
up, and it was reported she was going to end of track to see
Slade himself. Hard Sam also requested that Slade do nothing
about Flash Dan Delmont until he had sufficient help for the
job.

There was a grim expression on Slade's face as he screwed
up the paper and put it into a pocket. He pictured Maisie's
face, and guessed that Rolph had somehow learned the girl had
passed on the information about his hideout. If he could have
caught the payroll train he might have made it to end of track
before Rolph got there, and he clenched his teeth as he hoped
Maisie would have sense enough to remain under cover until he
arrived to protect her.

The train from El Paso pulled in and Slade stood alone on
the platform, waiting for Frank Burden to show himself. The
Area Manager alighted from the train and looked around,
shrugging his heavy shoulders when he saw Slade. Then came
forward, and he was a dozen yards away when he opened his
coat, revealing the gunbelt he was wearing. Slade saw nothing
ominous in the movement, but the next instant Burden was
making a fast draw, and there could be no mistake about the
Area Manager's intentions.

Slade was dimly aware that his right hand had darted to his
own weapon at the first sign of hostility. Burden was fast, his
gun clearing leather smoothly, and Slade dropped to one knee
as his .45 came to hand. Burden's gun crashed, spouting blue
smoke, and the bullet cut through the space where Slade's chest
had been a fraction of a second before. The slug crackled

through the air, missing Slade's head by a few inches. Hard on the heels of Burden's shot, Slade's gun blasted, and he aimed for a wing shot, not wanting to kill the Area Manager.

Burden took the bullet in the region of the right shoulder, and his gun fell from his hand. He twisted sharply, then sat down on the platform, but scrabbled around, reaching out for his weapon with his left hand. Slade ran forward, kicking the weapon clear, and his face was set like rock as he stared down at the pale faced Area Manager.

'Just what in hell was that all about?' Slade demanded. What happened in El Paso?'

'El Paso?' Burden gasped, his face grey with shock. His left hand was pressed to his bloodstained shoulder. 'It's what's been happening in Big Bend that's got me, Hollister. I got a wire from Lola this afternoon. She's run out on me. She said you're the man she's been fooling around with. It's always been you ever since before I married her.'

Slade gritted his teeth for a moment, recalling Lola as he had seen her that morning at Burden's house.

'What do you mean, she's run out on you?' he demanded. 'I was in Big Bend at dawn and she was there then. I spoke to her. She didn't say anything about leaving, and she sure didn't look ready to pull out. How would she go, and where to?'

'She took the midday train from here,' Burden said. 'I'm gonna kill you, Hollister. No matter what happens, I'll kill you for what you've done.'

'It's never been me with Lola,' Slade rasped. 'Phil Brady was the man you saw jumping out that coach window at end of track. I saw him and recognized him. He was here with Lola the night before, when he should have been meeting that gold shipment Rolph lifted when Harry Kelleher was killed. I don't know why Lola insists on getting you to think I'm the man fooling around with her, but I mean to find out, and when I've settled this business at end of track I'll go find Lola. I'll bring her back and we'll get the truth out of her.'

Burden shook his head. 'I'll ride with you to end of track.'

'You need medical treatment,' Slade retorted.

'You take a look at it. If Brady is at end of track then I got to talk to him.'

'If you're going to end of track then get aboard,' the con-

125

ductor said. 'We're running eight minutes late as it is.'

They boarded the train and made for the baggage car, where Slade examined Burden's wound. The bullet had missed the collar bone, but there was a nasty hole in the thick flesh just above it.

'I tried the best I could just to wing you,' Slade commented as he bandaged the wound. 'You're lucky I'm such a good shot. An inch lower and the Doc would have been cursing me for making such a mess of your shoulder. Now you better listen to what I've got to say, Frank, and take it in. I've repeated it often enough to you in the past but you won't have it. But I've got a lot to do at end of track and I don't want you getting in the way. You save your personal problems until after railroad business has been handled.'

'I'll go along with that,' Burden said through gritted teeth. His face was pale with shock. 'But I mean to get to the bottom of what's been going on.'

'That's my intention,' Slade retorted.

Night closed in as they reached the camp at end of track. Slade went forward to where he had left Burden, and the Area Manager was on his feet, his face pale, his teeth clenched. It was obvious he was barely hanging onto his senses. They looked at one another, and Burden grinned in what was a travesty of a smile.

'Stay out of it, Frank,' Slade warned as the train ground to a halt, and as the conductor thrust open a door they heard the sound of shots. 'What the hell.' Slade peered out into the night. There were fires burning in the camp. Someone had set fire to a stack of ties, and there were men standing around it like kids at a bonfire. Guns were being fired indiscriminately, but as far as Slade could tell there was no fight.

He jumped to the ground and started towards Chain Becker's coach, and had to push his way through a crowd of men all chanting and jeering. Becker himself was standing on the steps of his coach, trying to shout to the men, but they were making too much noise for his loud voice to be heard. Slade thrust his way to the steps and mounted to Becker's side.

'Thank God you're here,' Becker said, recognizing Slade in the faint light coming out of the coach.

126

'What in hell is going on?' Slade demanded. 'Are these men drunk already? How long have they been paid?'

'Paid? That's the whole trouble,' the camp boss replied. 'They haven't been paid. They're wrecking the camp because the payroll wasn't on the train.'

'It was.' Slade spoke through his teeth. 'Where's Phil Brady?'

'He disappeared in the camp before it was discovered that the payroll ain't aboard the train,' Becker said. 'There's a rumour that Drogo Rolph is around here.'

'Was the payroll stolen?' Slade could not understand what had happened.

'Must have been. The messenger on the train said the money was put in the safes in the express car, but when the safes were opened here at end of track they were empty. The money was gone.'

Slade stared at the camp boss in disbelief, and the shouting of the men dragged at his nerves.

'Get rid of these men,' he rapped. 'I'll get to the bottom of this. Where is the messenger?'

'In the coach here. Some of the men were talking about stringing him up. They figure he must have had something to do with the dough going missing.'

Slade went into the coach, and the messenger, who was sitting in a corner, started to his feet nervously. His face showed relief when he recognized Slade.

'Am I glad to see you,' he said. 'I'm afraid for my life. Those fools out there figure I helped steal that payroll.'

'How did it go missing?' Slade demanded. 'You were in the car all the time, weren't you?'

'We made an unscheduled stop for Phil Brady to get aboard the train,' the messenger said slowly. 'I left Brady in the express car. Hell, he's a company man. But those safes weren't damaged, Slade. Only a company man could have opened them without damaging them.'

'And Brady hopped off the train as soon as it got here, before the safes were opened and the money found to be missing, huh?' Slade's face seemed carved out of stone.

'That's right. I figure Phil Brady can do some explaining. I hope so because I sure as hell can't.'

Slade left the coach and paused at Becker's side. The camp boss had succeeded in quietening the men, but they were still standing in a sullen group, and their silence now seemed more ominous than the noise they had been making.

'Chain, did a girl show up here asking for me?' Slade demanded.

'Yeah. Come in from Jules Crossing. Said you would want me to take real good care of her.'

'Where is she now?'

'I put her in a tent. It's down there by the Chief Engineer's shack. She was scared as hell when she got in, Slade. But what about this payroll? What can we do about the men? They're gonna tear this camp to pieces if they can't buy liquor.'

'I'm going to close that saloon, so there'll be nothing for them to buy,' Slade retorted. 'Get your toughest men together, Chain. There must be some you can rely on. We're going to put Flash Dan Delmont out of business.'

Becker whooped with delight and yelled at the men.

'You want to get even with someone, don't you?' Becker demanded stridently. 'Delmont is the man causing all the trouble. He's laughing about it over in the saloon. Let's go over there and pay him a visit. It'll be drinks on the house, if you don't forget to take your axes and hammers and pick handles with you.'

A roar of approval rang out. Slade started across to the big tented saloon, and Chain Becker was at his side. By the time Slade was approaching the big tent most of the workers were behind him. He was swept into the tent on a human tide of determination and anger, which also pushed aside the hardcases Delmont had employed. There was a rush for the bar, and men began smashing at the gaming tables, the roulette wheels, anything they came across. Slade started the fight, but he did not join in. He slid to one side, ensured it was going well, then departed hurriedly. He had other things to do.

CHAPTER FIFTEEN

As he crossed the camp Slade glanced back at the saloon, where the uproar was swelling to the proportions of a riot. He passed the Chief Engineer's shack and found Maisie's tent. There was a lantern alight inside and he could make out two figures silhouetted against it. As he went nearer one of the figures ducked away from the other, and Slade saw a blow being struck. He took a quick breath as he entered the tent, and there he found Maisie cowering away from Flash Dan Delmont.

'What's going on here?' Slade demanded, and Delmont's face showed expression, for once losing its impassive blankness. 'Did you hit her, Delmont?' he asked softly.

Delmont cursed and reached inside his coat to his shoulder holster. Slade grinned, moving forward, not attempting to draw his holstered gun. He blocked Delmont's draw with his right hand, and slammed his left fist in a vicious arc, his hard knuckles smashing into Delmont's mouth. The saloonman fell away, but Slade kept after him, grabbing him, pulling him forward into more punishment, and he battered Delmont with both fists until the man crumpled in a state of insensibility.

'What was he beating you for, Maisie?' Slade demanded, breathing heavily, his anger still raging. He stared into the girl's battered face, noting the pallor, seeing relief, hope and fear mingled in her expression.

'Rolph is somewhere in the camp,' she cried. 'He means to get you as well as the payroll, Hollister. I saw Rolph in Jules Crossing, but got away before he could get to me. He's found out somehow that I told you about his hideout beyond Pinto Creek.'

'You got any idea where he is?' Slade demanded.

'No. I saw him with Mulie Johnson, but Becker put me in here, and I thought I was safe until Delmont came in. He's working in with Drogo, Hollister. He was gonna take me to Rolph, but he was trying to get me to tell him where you were hiding out.'

'Did he say where Rolph is?' Slade demanded harshly. 'I want to meet Rolph as much as he appears to want me. It's about time we settled this business.' He moved closer to the girl, looking at her bruises, and there was fear in her eyes.

'He didn't say. But I saw Brady in the camp. He was with the Burden woman, Slade. I heard them talking. Brady didn't know you'd been reinstated in your job until she told him. He figured he was still Chief Troubleshooter, but when she told him the truth he swore to kill you and her husband.'

'Lola Burden here in camp?' he demanded, frowning. 'Are you sure? Do you know her by sight?'

'Sure. It was her. I knew her a long time ago, before she ever married Frank Burden. She was in the same line of business I handled. She—' Maisie suddenly broke off, her face showing alarm. 'Look out,' she cried, and thrust at Slade, pushing herself in front of him.

Slade spun, his gun flashing into his hand, expecting to see someone coming into the tent. But it was Flash Dan Delmont unlimbering his .38 from its shoulder holster. Slade pushed his hand forward for a shot at the saloonman but Maisie was in the line of fire, and as he reached out his left hand to grab her Delmont cut loose. He fired three quick shots, his face twisted with hatred, his eyes wide with tension. The bullets struck Maisie, and as the girl went sprawling Slade sent a bullet through Delmont's head.

The tent seemed to reverberate to the shock of the gunfire, and Slade's ears were singing as he holstered his gun and bent over the inert girl. He turned her over gently, and a coldness seemed to close in around his heart when he saw that she was dead.

For some moments he stared down at her unseeingly. Then he drew a sharp breath and laid her down, straightening her body. He took a blanket from the camp bed and covered her over, and when he left the tent he did not even glance at the dead Flash Dan.

Slade walked unfeelingly towards Becker's coach on the loop. The payroll train was still standing in darkness on the main line, almost at the point where the track ended. He reached Becker's coach, but paused before entering, hearing a sound coming from the telegraph office nearby. There was a crashing sound, a shattering of glass, and Slade frowned as he eased his gun into his hand and started forward to investigate It sounded as if someone was smashing the telegraph.

Two figures appeared from the shack as Slade neared it, and he dropped to one knee. The figures paused, and Slade tried hard to make out details but could not.

'That will take care of the communications,' a man's voice said. 'Once we pull out on the train they won't be able to wire ahead to Las Corros and stop us.'

'But what about Frank, Phil?' a woman's voice demanded. 'He's here in camp. He got off that train with Hollister.'

Slade tightened his lips. That was Lola Burden. He wondered how she had managed to get to end of track from Big Bend without passing through Las Corros, and he knew from experience that she must have taken the down train to Redrock Canyon, then rented a buggy to cross the Sandstone Hills. She would have made it all right, and after sending that message to Frank Burden in El Paso she had pulled out to meet Phil Brady. But where was the payroll money? Brady had to know about that. He was the only man able to get at it.

'Brady,' he called as the two figures moved away from the shack. 'Hold it right there. This is Slade Hollister. I want you.'

Both figures halted, and then Brady was whirling to face Slade, his gun clearing leather. Slade thumbed off a shot that hit Brady somewhere chest high, spinning him around and dumping him on the ground. Lola turned instantly and ran, losing herself in the darkness. Slade let her go, knowing he could pick her up later without trouble. He ran forward to where Brady lay, taking up the man's discarded sixgun, dropping to one knee beside the inert figure.

'Are you hard hit, Phil?' Slade demanded harshly.

'You've done for me,' Brady retorted in gasping tones, his breathing harsh and rapid. 'Damn your hide, Slade. You always proved yourself better than me.'

'Tell me what's been going on, Phil.' Slade's voice was gentle. 'You can square yourself now. What about the payroll?'

'I got took by Rolph's gang when I chased them after their last raid,' Brady said hesitantly. 'Rolph and Mulie Johnson were waiting beside the track when I boarded the payroll train. I got the messenger to leave the express car, and opened the safes and passed the money to Rolph. They was gonna kill you in return for that payroll. I wanted your job permanently, Slade. I turned renegade to get the better of you, but you've done for me.'

'What about all the other gold shipments, Phil?' Slade asked. 'You passed on that information too, huh?' He felt Brady go limp and bent over the man. 'Phil tell me before it's too late. It was you passing on the information to Rolph all along, huh?'

There was no reply, and Slade shook his head slowly. He put his hand upon Brady's chest, feeling for a heartbeat, and there was nothing. Phil Brady was dead.

Leaving the body, Slade moved in the direction Lola had taken, and she came out of the shadows of Becker's coach as he reached it. Slade's sixgun leaped into his hand at her movement, but he holstered the weapon when he recognized her.

'I've got to talk to you, Slade,' she said hurriedly.

'Aren't you concerned about Brady?' he demanded. 'He was your lover. You wired Frank you were leaving him, telling him I was your man, but it was always Brady, wasn't it?'

'Brady.' There was scorn in her tones. 'I was only amusing myself with him. He pretended to be in love with me because he wanted my help to get your job. I pretended to be in love with him because I needed his help to get Frank moved out of this area. You wouldn't help me so I had to turn to someone.'

'Was Brady the renegade selling information to Rolph?' he demanded.

She laughed lightly. 'If you think that then you haven't got the sense I gave you credit for,' she retorted. 'Brady was after the renegade himself. He sometimes figured it was you or Hard Sam. He wanted to turn the renegade in to clinch getting the job of Chief Troubleshooter.'

'Then if it wasn't Brady it must have been Frank himself,' Slade spoke stiffly, his mind trying to work it out.

'That's right. It was Frank. That's why I've been trying to get him out of this area, away from Rolph's stamping ground. If you had helped me when I first asked you, Slade, there wouldn't have been half this trouble.'

'We'll go have a talk with Frank,' Slade said, taking hold of her arm. 'Come on. He'll be on the train we arrived in.'

'I don't want to face him, Slade,' she said, trying to pull away. 'After that wire I sent him, he'll kill me if he ever sets eyes on me again. He'll kill you too if you spring that business about him being a renegade. He's gone to a lot of trouble keeping it a secret. That was why I was making a run for it with Phil. We smashed the telegraph so Frank couldn't contact Las Corros before we reached there.'

'Sorry, Lola, but you got to face the consequences of your actions. I've still got an important chore to take care of. I heard Drogo Rolph is around here someplace, and I want to nail him.'

They had reached the side of the coach on the main line, and as Slade peered around a man moved out of the shadows on the observation platform, a gun glinting in his hand.

'So I got you dead to rights at last, Hollister,' he rasped. 'There you are, with your arm around my wife.'

Slade tightened his lips as he recognized Frank Burden's voice. He had been holding Lola's arm to prevent the girl running away. Now he let his arm fall to his side, and he faced Burden across the shadows that separated them.

'I'm holding Lola as a witness, Frank,' he said sharply. 'I guess you know why I want you. You're the renegade who's been passing information on the gold shipments to Drogo Rolph.'

'Are you crazy?' Burden demanded. 'Me? I figured it was you. It had to be you. It was you or Brady.'

Lola left Slade's side and walked to the steps of the coach, mounting them to her husband's side, and Slade stood thinking over Burden's words. But as soon as she was within arm's length of Burden, Lola grasped his gunarm, thrusting it upwards.

'Quick, Hollister!' she yelled. 'Shoot him. Kill him. He is the one been passing on the information.'

Burden yelled angrily and thrust his wife away. Slade did not wait but turned and faded swiftly into the shadows. He drew his gun as he dropped to one knee. But Burden was busily engaged with his wife, hitting Lola in the face to get her away from his gun. Lola suddenly slumped and Burden lifted her bodily and carried her into the coach. A few moments later Burden reappeared and went forward to the engine. He mounted to the footplate and the train began to move out.

Slade was undecided for a moment, but with Brady dead he knew the renegade had to be Frank Burden, and he wanted Burden. The Area Manager was obviously making a run for it, driving the engine himself, and Slade holstered his gun and leaped upon the rear platform as the train picked up speed. He peered through a window into the coach, seeing Lola lying on a couch. The woman was coming to, and Slade was about to go in to her when the door of the sleeping compartment was opened and a man appeared. Slade almost fell off the platform in surprise, for it was Drogo Rolph.

Rolph was carrying a bulging leather bag, which he set down, and while Slade could only stare, the outlaw gang leader helped Lola to her feet and took her into his arms. Shock was stabbing through Slade's mind, and all the unanswered questions that had been bothering him since the day he took over from his father now returned to add their confusion. Lola was acting like she knew Drogo Rolph.

Reaching for his gun, Slade was in the act of drawing the weapon when a terrific blow struck his shoulders. At first he thought the sky had fallen in upon him, and he staggered and went sprawling to the floor of the platform, almost pitching headfirst down the steps to the tracks dashing by beneath the clicking wheels. He gasped for breath as he grasped at the rail and began to haul himself upright, and as he turned to face the coach again a fist hit him in the face. He dimly saw the figure of a big man confronting him, and realized that he had jumped down from the roof of the car.

Acting instinctively, Slade steadied himself and ducked a following punch, then let go with a vicious uppercut that raked along the man's head. But it was like punching a wall, and Slade clenched his teeth at the pain in his hand. He changed his tactics as the man came boring in, sledging into the other's body, and as the train picked up speed they swayed and staggered perilously on the unsteady platform.

They rocked back and forth several times, grunting, cursing, punching and clawing, fighting for the advantage, and before many minutes had passed Slade was aware of the identity of his

134

attacker. It was Mulie Johnson. Realization brought despair, for Slade knew he could never beat this man in a stand up fight. Johnson was built like a mule and had about as much strength and endurance. His big fists dealt out punches that struck Slade as if they were kicks from the animal after which Johnson was nick-named.

But Slade was desperate. He brought up his knee as Johnson came at him again, sinking it into the man's belly, but Johnson merely grunted, and clipped Slade with a left and right to the head that made him see stars and coloured lights. Slade's knees began to buckle, and Johnson seized him, dragged his gun from its holster and sent it spinning away into the night, then thrust open the door of the coach and literally hurled Slade inside.

Rolph swung around from Lola, his gun appearing in his hand, but he relaxed when he saw Johnson standing behind the fallen Slade.

'He came sneaking onto the platform as the train pulled out, boss.' Johnson said laconically. 'I figured you might wanta see him before I throw him back off again.'

'I certainly do want to see him, Mulie,' Rolph said in harsh tones. 'It's Slade Hollister. I've been waiting a long time now to see him.'

Slade pushed himself into a sitting position, his senses whirling. 'No matter what you do to me now, Rolph,' he said. 'Phil Brady won't be able to step into my shoes. He's dead.'

'You've been busy, huh? That's okay. I don't need Brady. I don't need anyone any more. We got everything we want, and it's taken us a lot longer than we planned because of you and Hard Sam, Hollister.'

'Burden's driving the train,' Slade said. 'So he is the one who's been passing all the information about the gold shipments to you, huh, Rolph?'

'Frank Burden?' The gang boss grinned, his pale blue eyes over-bright. 'He never passed me a thing. Burden is railroad through and through. I didn't need Burden when he married my gal Lola.'

Slade looked at the woman. She was smiling, and she moved to Rolph's side and linked an arm through his. Her dark gaze was triumphant as she stared into Slade's face, drinking in his dazed expression.

'That's right, Hollister,' she said. 'I ran with Drogo before I ever came to the railroad. It was Drogo's idea that I should get someone like Frank Burden to marry me so I could get all the important information. Frank never knew what was going on. I played him for a sucker like I played every man I ever came across.'

'Except me, honey,' Rolph said, grinning. 'Okay, that's enough explaining. I waited a long time to face you, Hollister. You killed some of my men.'

'Most of the new gang you recruited,' Slade said, grinning. 'And Ned Bunch. You should have come yourself to do your own dirty work, Rolph. It might have been easier all round if you had. I even picked up Bull Seymour this morning. He hopped the train I was on outside Big Bend. He's in jail in Las Corros.'

'That must have been after he saw me,' Lola snapped. 'I told him about the payroll train.'

'And he got the message to me.' Rolph's eyes had hardened now, and he came to where Slade was sitting on the floor. 'It was a good thing we took Brady prisoner, huh? He agreed to give us that payroll in return for jumping you and finishing you off. Well we got the payroll. It's in that bag over there, and just because poor Brady is dead don't mean we ain't got to keep our bargain with him. On your feet, Hollister. I'm gonna kill you now. You're gonna get a slug in the guts. I know just where to put it so you'll take a long time to die. It's a good ride to Las Corros, and we're gonna sit around drinking, watching you die, Chief Troubleshooter.'

Slade steeled himself for the bullet, knowing he could expect no mercy. Even Lola was grinning expectantly. But behind the gang boss and the woman the door at the far end of the coach was opening slowly, and Frank Burden appeared, a gun in his hand.

'I've been listening, Rolph,' the Area Manager called, and he did not see the gun in Rolph's hand. 'So you figure to come out on top, huh?' He chuckled harshly. 'Not while I still control this area.'

Mulie Johnson uttered a bull-like roar and grabbed at the gun in his holster. Burden was grinning, his face a pale mask, and he fired two quick shots that filled the car with thunder and smoke. Johnson groaned and doubled up, his face twisting in agony, and his gun, which cleared leather, came spinning towards Slade. Rolph spun around at the shots and lifted his gun, triggering fast, sending a bullet into Burden's chest. Slade moved quickly, throwing a punch at the back of Rolph's neck, dropping the gang boss to one knee with the power of the blow.

Lola was screaming, the sound cutting shrilly through the blasting echoes of the shooting. Rolph turned, trying to bring his gun muzzle around to line up on Slade, who kicked out viciously, catching the man's wrist. The gun slipped from Rolph's grasp and went slithering away out of reach.

Rolph came to his feet like a mountain cat, and he was big, heavily built, a match for Slade. They fought tenaciously, rocking back and forth, swapping punches, kicking, gouging, and Rolph tried to sink his teeth into Slade's throat. They pounded one another with hard fists, struggling violently, and Rolph broke away and made a dive for his fallen gun. Slade jumped at him with both feet, sending him flying.

For long minutes that seemed to stretch into eternity they hammered at each other, grunting and cursing. Rolph caught Slade under the chin, hurling him backwards, sending him crashing over a chair, and as he got up again, Slade was remotely aware that the train was travelling too fast. Burden, lying dead in the doorway at the far end of the coach, must have left the throttle wide open. There was no one else on the footplate, and Slade turned cold inside as he realized that soon they would be hitting the three-mile grade. Once over that they would be tearing down the decline to Devil's Curve.

He saw Rolph diving once more for his gun, and levered himself upright, grabbing the chair that had tripped him and hurling it with all his strength at the outlaw. The chair crashed against Rolph and knocked him sideways. Slade went after him, glancing around, seeing Mulie Johnson lying apparently dead where he had fallen. Rolph came up to meet him, kicking aside the shattered chair, and there was a maniacal expression on the outlaw's face. He came for Slade with no guard up, intent upon seizing him by the throat. Slade hit him with a left hand that jolted him, but Rolph closed his hands around Slade's neck in a grip that would defy all attempts to break it. Slade went down on the floor, arching his back, dropping flat again and throwing himself over sideways. He slammed his fists into Rolph's face, smashing his knuckles against the big man's jaw.

Desperation seeped into Slade's mind. He could not break the madman's grip. His air was cut off. Black spots seemed to float before his eyes. Rolph was slobbering like a she-bear protecting a cub, a stream of curses bubbling from his slack lips. Slade could feel his senses failing. He thrust up his right hand, searching for Rolph's face, jabbing a stiffened thumb at the outlaw's right eye, gouging it in, feeling it jar against the socket. Rolph screamed hoarsely and flung himself away, breaking his grip on Slade's throat. Slade pushed himself into a sitting position, gasping for air, his shoulders heaving, his eyes almost glazed.

Rolph scrabbled for his gun. Slade pushed himself wearily to his feet. His attention was distracted from the outlaw by the fact that the train was climbing laboriously up a steep gradient. He knew exactly where they were and the knowledge gave him fresh stamina and desperate strength. When they reached the top of the rise they would plunge down the reverse slope to Devil's Curve, and if the brakes were not applied for most of that downward trip nothing could keep them on the rails at the curve.

He went after Rolph again, but at that moment Lola came towards him from the left. He looked at her quickly, intent upon getting to grips with the outlaw. Lola had a knife. Slade glimpsed something in her hand and thought it was a gun, and he was taken by surprise when she slashed at him instead of shooting. The long blade of the weapon sliced through the flesh of his left arm from elbow to wrist, laying it open almost to the bone. Blood spurted quickly and pain racked him.

Slade gritted his teeth, swinging his left hand. He gave Lola a back-hander that sent her sprawling, lifting her feet from the ground. He staggered to the right, catching his feet against the sprawled figure of Mulie Johnson, falling heavily. He did not take his eyes off Drogo Rolph, and saw the outlaw picking up his gun.

There were twenty feet between them as Rolph grasped the gun and turned to push himself to one knee. Slade was done. He could not get up. His right hand cast around, feeling for Johnson's discarded gun which he had seen fall close by. As Rolph struggled to bring his gun into the aim, Slade's fingers made contact with Johnson's weapon.

It was a purely instinctive movement. Slade did not realize that he had snatched up the gun until it blasted. He was mildly surprised as his right hand bucked a little, and he saw a red splotch appear on Drogo Rolph's forehead, the impact of the heavy bullet driving the man backwards.

Slade dropped the gun, levering himself to his feet, and he staggered and reeled to the doorway where Frank Burden lay inert. Blood was dripping from his split eyebrows. His knuckles and wrists ached. His left arm was leaking like a bucket with a hole in it. But none of these things made any impact upon his mind. He was only aware that the coach was tilting in the opposite direction, indicating that they had topped the rise and were moving down the grade to Devil's Curve. The rapid hammering of the wheels on the tracks warned him of their terrific speed, and he knew in one despairing moment of grim awareness that he could not possibly reach the engine in time to apply the brakes.

Looking around for Lola, he saw that she was moving towards Rolph, who lay upon his back with outflung arms. He went after her, his left arm useless, and when he grasped her she fought like a wildcat, clawing and scratching and reviling him.

'The train will jump the track at the bottom of the grade,' he shouted. 'Come on. We've got to get off.'

He dragged her to the door leading to the rear observation platform, but she was more than he could handle with his left arm useless. He had to let go of her while he dragged the door open, and she turned and ran back to where Rolph lay. Slade knew there was no time left. He staggered out to the platform, moved drunkenly down the steps and stuck his face out into the wind screaming past the car. There was no easy drop-off for him. Hard ground at the side of the track awaited his body. He hesitated, but the knowledge of what lay at the curve forced him to release his hold on the brass rail. He bent as low as he could, clenched his teeth, thrust with his legs, and pushed himself outwards away from the car.

139

Seconds later he hit the ground with a violent, bone-jarring impact, rolling over and over at the side of the track. He fetched up against a rocky slope, gasping and exhausted. In the distance the sound of the train continuing to hurtle down the slope came all too clearly on the night breeze. Slade pushed himself to his feet and staggered onto the track, staring down the grade. A thin crescent of the moon was peering from around a distant mountain peak. The train was a speeding black shadow moving to extinction. The twin rails vibrated loudly.

At the crucial moment Slade knew his worst fears were being realized. The train failed to take the bend. He watched in frozen horror, thinking of the woman still aboard, crouched by the side of a dead man while her husband lay nearby, uncared for and unloved.

The sounds of protesting metal came clearly to his ears as the engine and cars left the track. The engine raced all the faster with the friction gone from its wheels, and the tracks curved away from under it. The train continued in a straight line, sailing out into space and the dark night air.

For a moment it seemed to hesitate in its forward movement. Then it began to arc downward, slowly at first before dropping like a stone. Lights still blazed from the passenger car windows. Then there was a sudden silence, a heart-stopping moment of emptiness, followed by a never-ending, hollow-sounding crash of tortured metal and splintering wood. To Slade's imagination there seemed to come a trailing scream of human despair from the crash, although he knew it was impossible.

He stood unsteadily while he tied his neckerchief as best he could around his slashed left arm. There was not a part of his body that was free of pain, but he started down the grade, intent upon reaching the wreckage a hundred feet below Devil's Curve. His mind was curiously inactive now, and all the problems, the frustrations and irritations, were gone. As he reached the deadly curve in the track a locomotive came edging around it from the opposite direction, a yellow glare stabbing from its searchlight, picking out Slade's lone figure. The locomotive ground to a halt and figures descended from it, hurrying to surround him, and one of the first to arrive was Hard Sam, come to take a hand in the cleanup.

It was then Slade realized that it was all over bar the shouting and the writing of reports. He stiffened himself for the ordeal of talking about what had happened, and there were pictures in his mind of people – Maisie Clapham, Phil Brady, Frank Burden, Flash Dan Delmont and Drogo Rolph. They were done and gone, and he was still around. The Railroad was still there, and he was a railroad man. He had done his duty, completed the first job as Chief Troubleshooter in Hard Sam's place, and it weighed heavily upon his mind that it was merely the first of many such assignments.